THE
GODS
OF
EVERYTHING
ELSE
T. STYLES
NATIONAL BESTSELLING AUTHOR

CHECK OUT OTHER TITLES BY THE CARTEL PUBLICATIONS

SHYT LIST 1: BE CAREFUL WHO YOU CROSS
SHYT LIST 2: LOOSE CANNON
SHYT LIST 3: AND A CHILD SHALL LEAVE THEM
SHYT LIST 4: CHILDREN OF THE WRONGED
SHYT LIST 5: SMOKIN' CRAZIES THE FINALE'
PITBULLS IN A SKIRT 1
PITBULLS IN A SKIRT 2
PITBULLS IN A SKIRT 3: THE RISE OF LIL C
PITBULLS IN A SKIRT 4: KILLER KLAN
PITBULLS IN A SKIRT 5: THE FALL FROM GRACE
POISON 1
POISON 2
VICTORIA'S SECRET
HELL RAZOR HONEYS 1
HELL RAZOR HONEYS 2
BLACK AND UGLY
BLACK AND UGLY AS EVER
MISS WAYNE & THE QUEENS OF DC
BLACK AND THE UGLIEST
A HUSTLER'S SON
A HUSTLER'S SON 2
THE FACE THAT LAUNCHED A THOUSAND BULLETS
YEAR OF THE CRACKMOM
THE UNUSUAL SUSPECTS
LA FAMILIA DIVIDED
RAUNCHY
RAUNCHY 2: MAD'S LOVE
RAUNCHY 3: JAYDEN'S PASSION
MAD MAXXX: CHILDREN OF THE CATACOMBS (EXTRA RAUNCHY)
KALI: RAUNCHY RELIVED: THE MILLER FAMILY
REVERSED
QUITA'S DAYSCARE CENTER
QUITA'S DAYSCARE CENTER 2
DEAD HEADS
DRUNK & HOT GIRLS
PRETTY KINGS
PRETTY KINGS 2: SCARLETT'S FEVER
PRETTY KINGS 3: DENIM'S BLUES
PRETTY KINGS 4: RACE'S RAGE
HERSBAND MATERIAL
UPSCALE KITTENS
WAKE & BAKE BOYS
YOUNG & DUMB
YOUNG & DUMB: VYCE'S GETBACK
TRANNY 911
TRANNY 911: DIXIE'S RISE
FIRST COMES LOVE, THEN COMES MURDER
LUXURY TAX
THE LYING KING
CRAZY KIND OF LOVE
SILENCE OF THE NINE
SILENCE OF THE NINE II: LET THERE BE BLOOD
SILENCE OF THE NINE III
PRISON THRONE
GOON

Hoetic Justice
And They Call Me God
The Ungrateful Bastards
Lipstick Dom
A School of Dolls
Skeezers
Skeezers 2
You Kissed Me Now I Own You
Nefarious
Redbone 3: The Rise Of The Fold
The Fold
Clown Niggas
The One You Shouldn't Trust
Cold As Ice
The Whore The Wind Blew My Way
She Brings The Worst Kind
The House That Crack Built
The House That Crack Built 2: Russo & Amina
The House That Crack Built 3: Reggie & Tamika
The House That Crack Built 4: Reggie & Amina
Level Up
Villains: It's Savage Season
Gay For My Bae
WAR
WAR 2
WAR 3
WAR 4
WAR 5
WAR 6
WAR 7
Madjesty vs. Jayden
You Left Me No Choice
Truce: A War Saga (War 8)
Truce 2: The War Of The Lou's (War 9)
An Ace And Walid Very, Very Bad Christmas (War 10)
Truce 3: Sins of The Fathers (War 11)
Truce 4: The Finale (War 12)
Ask The Streets For Mercy
Treason
Treason 2
Hersband Material 2
The God's Of Everything Else (War 13)
The End. How To Write A Bestselling Novel in 30 Days

WWW.THECARTELPUBLICATIONS.COM

THE GOD'S OF EVERYTHING ELSE: AN ACE AND WALID SAGA

By

T. STYLES

PUBLISHER'S NOTE:
This book is a work of fiction. Names, characters, businesses,
Organizations, places, events and incidents are the product of the
Author's imagination or are used fictionally. Any resemblance of
Actual persons, living or dead, events, or locales are entirely coincidental.

Library of Congress Control Number: 2021925342

ISBN 10: 1948373769

ISBN 13: 978-1948373760

Cover Design: BOOK SLUT CHICK

First Edition

Printed in the United States of America

What Up Famo,

First off, I gotta say HAPPY BIRTHDAY to the QUEEN, Toy Styles! If the eBook version of this novel dropped into your DM on the actual release date, it's January 31, 2022, which is Mama T's birthday! Make sure you slide by any one of her social media pages and give her some love!

I am in such an amazing place right now. It's new book drop day, I finally finished my long anticipated follow up novel last month and dropped it, so if you haven't already go get, Hersband Material 2 because its live. Also, my pooh's birthday and my sister CeCe is making MAJOR strides in her ongoing recovery, so life is UP and continuing to climb. Thank you all who have kept her in prayer because its working.

Now, onto the book in hand, THE GOD'S OF EVERYTHING ELSE! Mannnnn, you know how sometimes you don't realize how much you love or miss something until its gone? Well, that's where I was until T dropped this book. I have absolutely missed my folks and when I went through this tale, I had ALL the feels of the Wales and Louisville clan right back! You guys are in for a MAJOR treat, so enjoy!!

With that being said, keeping in line with tradition, we want to give respect to a vet, new trailblazer paving the way or pay homage to a favorite. In this novel, we would like to recognize:

Betty White

Betty Marion White was an American actress, comedian, humanitarian, and animal welfare advocate. In a documentary based on her life and career, she was referred to as the "First Lady of TV". She has had several movies and shows on television dating back to 1945. But out of EVERYTHING I've seen her in, besides the movie, The Proposal because she was hilarious, my favorite role was Rose Nyland in The Golden Girls! I remember being about 13 or 14 years old and watching the show with my grandmother. I laughed just as hard as my grandma did even though I was young. That's great comedy!

Betty White was passionate about animals, a supporter and advocate of LGBT and civil rights, Betty was an all-around beautiful human and when she took her last breath on December 31, 2021, after living 99 years and 348 days, it seemed as though it still was too soon. Thank you for being a friend Mrs. White. We love you!

My apologies for the long letter, but I didn't get a chance to holla at my folks in our last drop as T penned that one, so I had something to say. LMAO!

Aight nah, goin' and get to it, the Wales' and Lou's are waiting!

Love y'all!
Charisse "C. Wash" Washington
Vice President
The Cartel Publications
www.thecartelpublications.com
www.facebook.com/publishercwash
Instagram: Publishercwash
www.twitter.com/cartelbooks
www.facebook.com/cartelpublications
www.theelitewritersacademy.com
Follow us on Instagram: Cartelpublications

#CartelPublications

#UrbanFiction

#PrayForCece

#RIPBettyWhite

#THEGODSOFEVERYTHINGELSE

PROLOGUE – TUESDAY
MANY YEARS LATER

The night sky was spectacular for Ace and Walid's eighteenth birthday party. Stars sparkled and the ocean sang as beautiful women with brown skin and long black flowing hair danced for their attention.

Behind the ladies sat a band, which played the twins favorite songs. They were doing the job so well; one could hardly tell the original from the cover.

It's true, Banks and Mason didn't hold back a stack when it came to ushering their spawn into adulthood.

Gone were the boys of yesteryear.

The twins had transformed and become men so exotic looking, that both sexes did double takes when witnessing their beauty.

With time's blessing, Ace and Walid had turned into tall muscular men with skin, literally the color of golden sand. Every inch of their bodies were covered in tribal tattoos and their long black curly hair was gold at the tips, healthy and shiny.

Per usual, Ace wore his mane wild and out of control while Walid preferred to tame his with a gold hair band.

Walid was muted in his clothing choices. Preferring the comfort of linen or no shirt at all.

But Ace longed for the rich, hood nigga life and the gold and diamond chain draped around his neck that read *I AM GOD* told the world about his hidden desire for power, money, and everything in between.

They looked like stars.

And to the islanders they were.

But more things than just their bodies changed over the years.

Walid met the love of his life. He referred to her as his wife. She was a beautiful island girl who had given birth to his son, Baltimore Wales. Walid loved his family truly and had grown to become a man of honor, code and generosity.

In fact, it was whispered that his only weakness was his brother.

And unfortunately for Walid, that was the most dangerous weakness to possess.

Ace was an entirely different person all together.

If being accurate was a requirement, he would be considered a monster.

Ace was more selfish than a Pitbull being asked to share from his bowl. Meaner than a rattle snake and as sneaky as a stickup kid watching a block nigga pocket his cash after a night's work.

Sure, they had the same faces.

But they didn't share the same hearts.

The only positive attribute Ace possessed was the complete love he had for his twin, even though his actions often said differently.

But tonight, it was a celebration.

For darkness was at bay.

Well, not really.

As the twins sat on gold and black throne chairs and watched a group of beautiful women dance for them in the sand, Ace sighed and sunk deeper into despair. His desire to taste blood was growing by the second.

"What's wrong, brother?" Walid asked, leaning to the right. Shirtless, his muscles buckled under the moonlight.

Ace sighed. "Do you ever get tired of it all?" He readjusted his dick to the left.

"Of what?"

"Of having everything and nothing at the same time." When he saw one of the dancers gawking, he shoved his button-down shirt to the left and right, as if he was opening curtains, just to be sure his jewels shined through.

Walid looked to his left at his girlfriend who played with his son and exhaled. "Nah, I like not having to worry about anything. I like knowing that my family is safe. I'm at peace, brother. And I wish you could be too."

His girlfriend winked at her man.

He winked back.

Ace glared.

He hated when his brother sounded what he deemed as weak.

"That's because you got a girl and my nephew," he continued. "But what I got? Nothing. And I need something of my own." He focused on the only beauty amongst the dancers who refused to give him eye contact.

"You got a lot. You had a few women too, but you always cut them off when they want you to commit." He laughed. "Maybe you need adventure. Pops and Uncle Mason said we can take a trip to—."

"Another island! I'm tired of going to other islands!"

"Then, where you wanna go?"

"America! Where we were born!"

Walid sat back as if he just said fighting words. "They said we would never be able to go back there. You know that. And to be honest, based on what we see on the news I don't want to. Maybe—."

"I know what they said! But I'm sick of following their rules!"

A few people paused to see what the princes were yelling about.

"But what about what we want, brother?" Ace waved one of their employees over. "Tell that girl to come over here. The one with the heart tattoo on her wrist."

"Sure boss."

When the employee whispered to the girl, she looked at Ace and shook her head. Sadly, the employee approached having unfulfilled his request. "She said no. Did you want one of the other young ladies? One of them seems to be quite smitten with you. I can—."

"Do you work for her or me?" He glared up at him.

"Leave it alone, brother," Walid said.

"You know what, I'll do it myself. I'll be right back." Ace rose yanked off his shirt and dropped it on the beach. Storming over to the dancers, he kicked up sand like smoke trails from speeding tires.

The *I AM GOD* medallion glistened against his chiseled chest.

And yet he looked like a beautiful devil.

Grabbing the girl by the arm, he yanked her over to the towel shack as they both disappeared inside.

It was caveman style.

Walid grew uneasy wondering what was going on while also knowing that in Ace's mind he could be, have and do whatever he wanted. The island was literally named, Wales Island.

And they were island princes.

So, didn't that mean they were invincible?

Ace certainly thought so.

Fifteen minutes later as the band continued to play, the beautiful island girl with the heart tattoo came running out of the shack, her clothing hanging off her arm. She was also partially covered in blood.

A few seconds later, Ace exited adjusting his linen pants. Scratches were all over his bare chest and a blood drop sat on his diamonds.

Flopping on his throne he looked over at his brother and grinned. "I'm bored, Wally. I need an escape."

"What did you do?" Walid glared.

"What I always do. Took what I wanted." He placed a heavy hand on his shoulder. "Now do your job and go clean up my mess." He winked. "I know you can never help yourself."

"Be careful with me, brother." Walid warned. "You won't get away with how you moving in life for long."

Ace winked. "I guess we gonna see."

CHAPTER ONE
WALID

"Monsters rarely change forms."

The wind washed back and forth on the beach, as Walid paced around his bedroom within the Wales Mansion. The large floor to ceiling windows were open and did nothing to soothe the anger circulating through his heart.

After witnessing Ace shame the island girl by once again taking whatever he wanted, he started to hate his brother's ways. Hating the man himself would be difficult, after all he was his twin.

Literally they entered the world together.

And not many people could say the same. But it didn't mean he agreed with his actions.

He was just about to open the window to allow the breeze to come through when his girlfriend entered. Her long hair curled in a lock formation towards the end. It ran down her back and made her look animated.

Doll like.

He fucking loved her.

The moment they met each other it was obvious that she would be his, despite a rocky start. Even Banks and Uncle Mason, who preferred to be called

Pops, saw the passion brewing between them despite others feeling differently. She was stunning for sure, but it was her soft nature and gentle spirit that calmed and soothed Walid.

She had a knack of being there always when he wanted or needed her the most.

"Our son…is he sleep?"

"Yes." Her voice was just above a whisper and blended in with the sound of the sea.

He nodded. "Tonight…" He dragged his hand down his face. "It's not what I wanted. And I'm sorry you had to see the girl hurt."

"Is she okay?"

He sighed. "She was shaken. And I can tell, although I wanted to help her and make sure she was fine, that my face…my face…"

"Reminded her of him."

Silence.

"That's a curse when he acts this way," she continued. "You literally can't tell you apart."

"He'll change. I keep holding on to the hope that…"

"He will never change. Monsters rarely change form." She moved closer. "Walid…I…hate to add more to your plate but…"

He moved closer. "What is it?"

"Before I say what I'm about to say, I want you to remember that you have the choice to let your brother handle his own trouble. It's time to let him reap what he sows instead of always coming to the–."

"What's wrong?"

"The police. They're here. And I told your fathers."

CHAPTER TWO
BANKS WALES
"I have many."

Age looked good on *Banks the Billionaire* despite the rage on his handsome face. Wearing a white short-sleeved shirt, unbuttoned and exposing the various tattoos displayed on his body, he stormed toward his destination. The white matching shorts exposed his muscular tatted legs which buckled with each stomp.

As he rushed down the corridor of the Wales Estate on his beautiful island, six men followed him eager to do whatever Banks required.

And when we say anything, we mean anything.

He was sick of those who refused to let him live in the peace he had envisioned for himself.

Dragging his hand backwards through his salt and pepper curly hair, he tried to reason what to do with his youngest son. He was done with moments like this. Where he would be forced to bail him out of another problem.

And yet, deep in his soul he realized that both he and Mason created the madness. He didn't want his children to have to worry about finances or where they were going to sleep or live. And so, he overindulged all six of them by not only giving them anything their heart desired but also by coming to the rescue on more than one occasion.

And now due to his financial affections, one of his children was quite literally spiraling out of control.

"When we get to the door don't say anything." Banks said to his men, scratching the old scar on his face that he gained many years ago as a young man. "I'll handle everything."

"What about Mason?" One of his men whispered.

"Does he already know?"

"Yes, sir. Aliyah told him earlier."

He shook his head. The last thing he needed was him mixing in. Besides, they had quite different approaches on how to raise Ace and Walid, the children they shared together.

And to think, it wasn't supposed to be that way.

Banks had frozen his eggs and was going to have Mason's ex-wife, at the time, carry it as they were a couple. But Mason, consumed with jealousy, got wind of the plan and inserted his sperm for the donor, resulting in Ace and Walid Wales being born of Wales and Louisville blood.

Mason preferred to let their sons learn their own way while Banks took the, I'll do whatever I can to save them approach. And although they were now eighteen it was quite obvious that Ace was out of touch with reality.

Mason also believed that empowering his kids to understand that they could have and do anything they wanted would make them stronger.

While Banks preferred the approach showing them that it was better to be well-rounded. And that power, *real* power, was always silent.

"I'll deal with Mason later." Banks said.

When they arrived at the door, the butler was waiting.

Banks nodded, giving permission to open the door. With the night sky as the backdrop, on the other side, four men stood, all wanting their attention.

While they couldn't be called police, it was obvious that the one closest to the door was in charge.

"Mr. Wales." He nodded. His face was wrinkled and in the shape of an egg.

"How can I help?" Banks asked firmly.

"Is your son here?"

"I have many."

The man smirked. "One of the twins. I believe his name is Ace."

"What do you want with him?"

"A young girl. An islander's daughter made some very serious accusations. So, we won't be long, but this has to be addressed. Now where is he?"

Banks stepped closer. "I still don't get what you want with my son."

"I'm sorry. I thought I made myself clear, as you are a very intelligent and wealthy man." It was obvious that he, like some, felt Banks' wealth afforded him a lifestyle that people born there should receive. "We want to question him."

Banks readjusted his stance and crossed his arms over his chest. "Does the commissioner know you're here?" It was time to go the fuck over his head.

He cleared his throat. "I don't see how that makes any difference."

"And yet I'm waiting on an answer."

"Uh, no, sir. He isn't aware."

"Well, maybe we should get him involved. He's good with clearing up misunderstandings." Banks turned around and looked at one of his men who was already on his phone.

With an extended hand the man said, "There's no reason to call my boss."

"Are you sure?" Banks threatened.

"No...please don't do that."

Banks shook his head and his man put the cell phone back into his pocket. Focusing forward he said, "I'm not sure what occurred tonight, but I'm certain that it's nothing I can't handle."

"May we talk frankly?" The man asked.

Banks nodded.

"I've seen the one you call Ace roaming about the islands. Unlike the other twin, his heart is dark. He grabs food off the tables of farmers who toil and work all day. He walks into the house of anybody with an open door and makes himself welcome at their tables. He throws the idea of money and power around as if he's God himself."

The embarrassment Banks felt in that moment was too great. This was certainly not a representation of the man he wanted to raise.

Why was Ace insistent upon doing bamma shit?

"Your point?"

"My point is that your money will not help this time."

Banks had proven over and over that throwing millions around worked every fucking time, so he was curious. "Why do you say that?"

"The girl was raped."

Outside Banks was as cool as an air conditioner blowing at fifty degrees on full blast. But inside he was furious. If it were true that his son was a rapist, this would not go over easy.

He would see to it!

"My son is not a rapist."

"And yet here we are, coming to you about rape."

Banks glared with one step forward. "Be easy with me."

He swallowed. "Sir, I am trying my level best."

"Who is the young girl's father?"

"You don't know him. He doesn't live on your island."

"Of course not. But it doesn't mean I can't speak with him."

Banks owned the entire island his mansion sat on which was vast. And to get to his shores, you had to fly or take a boat. Which meant most of the people who tended to his land lived on the surrounding island of Pearl in Belize.

"Now, who is her father?" Banks continued.

"He grows corn and rice. In a small town next to Pearl called Majorca."

Banks knew exactly who he was. "Let him know that one of my men will be coming to see him in the next few days." The plan was to give him enough money so that he nor his daughter would ever have to work a day in their lives again.

"What is the reason for–."

"My reasons are my own."

"Money doesn't get you out of everything you know."

"Says the man who is poor." Banks smiled and closed the door. He was no longer interested in taking an audience.

But the moment it was shut, rage took over his disposition as he rushed to find Ace.

MASON LOUISVILLE
MOMENTS EARLIER

Just like Banks and Mason did when life became a struggle, Ace took solace sitting next to the orange glow of the fireplace. It didn't matter that the island's temperature never went below seventy degrees, in that room they blasted the air to justify sitting next to the fire's warmth.

And it was there that he stood, looking down at the wood crackling, while Mason sat in a soft burgundy leather armchair. His black cane lying next to his leg.

Many years back, his ex-wife Jersey, who was Banks' woman at the time, shot him, resulting in him not being able to use his legs. Many thought he would never walk again. But Banks' money and focus afforded him the best care and as a result, with the exception of a slight limp, his gait was fine.

Although age settled in on his face just like with Banks, neither showed any real signs with the exception of the snowflakes that dusted their black manes. Wearing gold enhanced Versace baroque shorts and a black shirt unbuttoned once at the top, he looked like money.

Let's keep it one hundred.

The Baltimore natives looked the fuck good, and it was clear to all that they were a different breed.

As Ace gazed at the glow of the flames, his shirt hung open. Under the light Mason could see signs of scratches as well as a dip of blood on his diamond chain.

Although angry, Mason would often find himself mesmerized at how beautiful his and Banks' DNA mixed to create the twins. And in his silent opinion, their lives were his best work.

Rubbing his goatee, Mason sighed deeply. "You ever heard of the story of Icarus?"

He looked at him once. "No, pops."

He sighed. "Well Icarus was the son of a master craftsman. One day Icarus and his father attempted to flee from the town they were in, using the wings that the craftsman made."

Ace looked at him. "What happened?"

"Well, the craftsman warned his son not to fly too low or too high. He said the sea could dampen his wings while the sun would melt them."

Ace sighed. "So, what did he do?"

"Icarus didn't listen. He flew close to the sun and drowned in the sea."

Ace caught where he was going.

"Did you fly too close to the sun, Ace?"

Silence.

"When are you going to tell me what happened?" Mason continued. "We've been in here for almost an hour and yet you haven't said a word."

Ace looked at the fireplace and then back at Mason. "You told me that I could always have what I wanted."

Mason took a sip of the finest whiskey and sat the glass down on the table.

Many years ago, Mason gave up drinking. But after he was shot and almost tortured to death by his ex-Dasher, he picked up his glass again.

"It's true." He said to his son.

"Well, if that's the case, why is everyone upset tonight?"

"Ace, you still haven't told me what occurred. Why?"

"Because I don't...I don't want you to think differently about me."

"In a moment Banks will be here. Don't leave me ill informed."

Ace looked at the fireplace once more. His heart pounded just hearing what he already knew to be true. In the mansion, *Banks was coming*, were literally fighting words for him.

"He doesn't like me."

"You sound like a fool. You're his flesh and blood. And if you want me on your side then you'll have to tell me the truth."

"Will you be able to handle it?"

"Ace..."

He swallowed. "There was this girl. A girl that wanted me."

"If she wanted you, there is no problem."

"I'm not saying that it is! You must listen so you'll hear the rest."

Mason leaned forward. In Ace's mind his fathers were older, and he could have his way if he tried. But he had no idea about their dark pasts, or he would have humbled himself immediately. "Be easy, boy."

He looked down. "I meant no disrespect."

"Then prove it."

"There was this girl. I knew she wanted me, and I wanted her. She just needed a little help."

Mason glared. "I don't understand."

"Well, you see, I approached her after seeing her look my way. We went to the towel shack." He shrugged. "Had sex. But then she went crazy and started scratching up my chest."

"Are you telling me that you raped someone?" Mason's heart thumped powerfully.

Mason was sexually abused as a child and rape was the one area in his life that even at this moment brought him great disdain. He would write off anyone who took another sexually without approval even his own son.

"Sir, she wanted me. And then she went off in an attempt to blackmail me. She said she and her father would gain wealth off of me. That's all I can say."

Before Mason could dig deeper, Banks rushed into the lounge. Concerned, Mason grabbed his cane and rose. Standing next to Ace he positioned himself as if he was his lawyer, preparing to defend him at all costs.

Walid also entered.

The four of them, skin glowing in the darkened room as if they had been dusted with gold, stared at one another.

And all wanted answers.

"Hear him out first." Mason said firmly.

Banks rushed toward Ace. Standing in his face he asked, "Is it true?"

"Father, I don't know what you heard."

"I'm getting tired of all your games." His breath rose up and down in his chest. "Now tell me what fucking happened!"

"There was this chick at the party."

"Chick? Since when you call women chicks?" Banks asked.

"There was this woman, about my age. And...and she was eyeing me. So, we went to the towel shack and did our thing. I mean what she trying to say? Because I'm the one with scratches all over me."

He raised his arms to the sides, as if niggas couldn't already see the shit.

Walid looked away, having witnessed the entire ordeal go down.

"I don't believe you." Banks looked at Walid for answers instead. "Tell me what happened, son. So, I can get ahead of this."

Walid looked Banks into his eyes. "You know I can't do that, father." He focused on Ace. "He's my brother."

Banks glared. "When are you going to realize he's not your responsibility?"

"Maybe we can learn together."

Wrong answer.

Mason looked down and Banks shoved Walid across the room. "Come again."

Walid readjusted his stance. "I mean no disrespect, father. You know I don't. But he's my brother and I won't get in the middle of this. Please don't try and make me."

Banks took a deep breath and focused back on Ace. At least he could understand where Walid was coming from.

But Ace was another thing altogether.

"For the next week you will remain in this house." He pointed at the floor. "You will not leave these doors. Not even to look at sand. The only place you will be allowed to take fresh air is on the patio connected to your room. Everything else concerning you will remain in these walls." He stepped closer. "If I find out that you disobeyed me, you'll see a side of me you won't like. Don't test me."

Ace stormed away.

Mason stood in front of his oldest, truest friend. Their history ran so deep it couldn't be placed into words. The bond they shared welded them together in love, respect and adoration.

Yet on this they disagreed.

"Are you going to ask my opinion?" Mason questioned.

"No. His warped view of life is mostly your fault." He pointed at him.

"So, I'm the one that whisked all of us away and bought an island?" He placed a hand on his chest. "Lacing it with every pleasure known to man? Including the company of many women?"

"No. You're the one who warped his mind. I told you convincing him he could do anything was trouble. Besides, the only billionaire in this bitch is me."

Mason glared. "Age has made you arrogant."

"Age has made me wiser." Banks looked at Walid. "Go check on the band that played for your party. Make sure they have everything they need in their quarters. They will be here for a few days. Also see if they saw anything. I don't need them talking about what they've learned when they get back to the states."

"Yes, sir." Walid turned to walk away and then returned. "And fathers, I'm sorry."

Banks kissed him on the forehead.

Mason touched his back.

Walid walked away.

Banks and Mason looked at one another.

It was obvious that they literally created a monster in Ace. A mixture of what was good and bad about both of them coursed through Ace's veins. And neither could see anything positive happening anytime soon.

"It won't always be like this." Mason promised.

Banks wished that were true. "How can you be sure? Tell me something, Mason. Because when I look into his eyes...it..."

Banks feared only two things in life. Something happening to his family, which included Mason and the remaining Louisville spawn.

And Ace's reckless behavior.

"It's true, Banks. He will come around. But he won't let you apply pressure for long. And because of it, he will make moves to find his own way. Moves you won't like."

"I won't allow it," Banks said seriously.

"It doesn't make it untrue."

"How do you know he'll come around?" Banks said.

"Because we did the same thing to our fathers. He'll buck all of your rules and he'll pay. And his fall will be bad. And that's when the transformation will begin."

"This is reckless talk! Do you know he walks into the homes of people without an invitation? Fuck is wrong with him?"

"You want to save him from the monster he is. I want him to live fully in the monster he has become. Because only then will he truly find his own way."

CHAPTER THREE
ACE

"I see you."

Ace sat on the edge of his bed looking out the window which, like all the rooms in the mansion, stretched from one side of his massive bedroom to the next. He could still see where the ocean and golden sand met even though it was pitch black outside.

He was also enraged.

He couldn't understand why he was told from one parent that anything he wanted was his and that the other parent didn't seem to feel the same. He loved them both equally but was growing tired of Banks' oppressive rules.

And dare he say, tired of paradise.

But there was something else that he was longing for. Although he was nowhere near being able to articulate it so clearly, there was a part inside of him that wanted to experience what Walid had.

A love so focused on him that he could breathe a new life simply by looking into her eyes.

Sure, he had women who came in and out of his orbit at one point or another. And they were all beautiful in their own right. But he was also aware that they knew of Banks' power.

Of Banks' fortune.

Secretly he resented Banks' influence. And how everyone on the surrounding islands were fully aware that with one call, Banks could make anyone, or any situation disappear.

So, could he, the son of a king, experience *true* love under such circumstances?

He reasoned not.

He was still in his own mind when he felt a set of warm hands cover his eyes. Along with her budding breasts pressing against his back he could also smell the scent of vanilla and sugar on her skin. Which was her favorite fragrance.

"Guess who." She said playfully.

Ace knew who it was but also realized that this particular person enjoyed this game. Despite having played it a million times he continued to pretend to be clueless.

"Let's see, is it Minnesota?"

"No," she giggled.

"Is it Aliyah?"

"No silly."

"Is it Blakeslee?"

Having answered his sister correctly, she removed her hands and stood in front of him in all her Wales splendor.

This moment definitely deserves a pause because to explain her beauty inaccurately would be an injustice. There weren't the right words to say how drop-dead gorgeous 15 1/2-year-old Blakeslee Wales had gotten over the years.

A lover of the sun her naturally yellow tones were dusted with what could be described as a cinnamon complexion. Her hair fell into unraveled curls that draped over her shoulders and touched the small of her back. Her eyes were as wide as an anime doll and were framed with rows of naturally long eyelashes.

There were few women on planet Earth that would be considered the most beautiful. But if there was a competition, she would come close to winning.

Wearing a red cami with blue shorts, she squeezed her hands in front of herself and moved repeatedly as if she had to go to the bathroom. "Well?"

"What you doing up?"

"You know, silly."

"What do you want to know?" He grabbed her hand and she sat sideways on his lap.

"How was the party? You promised to tell me everything."

Up until that moment he wasn't in a good mood. He was mad at everybody but Walid. But if family members could be considered fans, he was it for Blakeslee. Because she thought Ace was the coolest person that was ever born. And her undying love for her brother, made her highly suggestable to his bad habits.

But please be clear, he loved his little sister dearly.

And would cause anyone great harm who meant to disrespect her. And that went for all of her brothers too.

"To be honest, B, I don't want to talk about it."

She eased off his lap. "But you promised."

"Blakeslee, listen to me. I would have had a better time staying here with you and eating the cake you made for me."

Her face lit up with joy. "Really? Even though it was lopsided?"

He chuckled. "Yes. Because you made it for me." He placed a hand over his heart.

"Then why didn't you stay? Because I get so bored in this house. Father doesn't let me go or do anything. I'm not even allowed to look at the internet. Even when the teachers come, they turn off access." She said quietly. "So, when you tell me the stories...I...I light up."

"I know but I promise you this. When we get older I'm going to show you adventures that you can't even imagine out in the world. Away from the island."

"Really?"

"Trust me."

Those were words she would hold him to.

She moved anxiously again and allowed her hand to disappear behind her back and into her pocket. With a tug and light pull, she removed a small box. It was black and crossed down the middle with a golden bow.

Ace smiled. "For me?"

"Who else, silly?"

Taking his sweet time to examine the box, he grinned. Looking up at her he said, "You know, this is the first gift I got today."

"But Father–"

"Yes, father threw me the party. And put some money in my bank account. And yes Walid bought me a pair of Yeezy's I wanted. And yes pops went out and brought the most beautiful women around to come to our event. But this is the first gift that came in a box with a bow. So, it means more."

She wrapped her arms around his neck and squeezed. Her hair dusted the side of his face, and he inhaled her innocent and untouched love. When he finally found a woman, if she didn't love him as much as his sister, he didn't want her.

"Now open it!" She said clapping once.

He raised the lid and inside was a small gold bracelet. It was made for the wrist. Everybody in the Wales clan knew Ace loved jewelry. But normally he liked it big and gaudy. And yet nothing was more beautiful than the jewelry in his hand.

Inscribed on the inside of the golden band were the words they always said to one another...*I SEE YOU.*

Overflowing with excitement she removed the bracelet from him and placed it on his wrist. "Promise me you'll never take it off, Ace."

"I'll kill before I let somebody take this away."

She sighed deeply. "I love you."

"I love you more."

She took another long breath. "I don't know what's wrong with you. But your sadness makes me weak, so I won't stay much longer. I just want you to know that I know you're not mean. I know you aren't selfish. And I know you're a good person."

As she walked to the door Ace said, "So, what did you get Walid?"

"Nothing. He got everything already." She shrugged.

When she disappeared, he thought about what she said. She was speaking gospel because his brother did have the dream.

The wife.

The baby.

The love.

But what also rang in his head was who in the household was calling him selfish? Who was calling him mean? And who was talking behind his back?

The unanswered questions swirled through his mind.

And for the moment, kept him company.

CHAPTER FOUR

WALID

THE NEXT MORNING

"Why are you always in Wales business?"

Walid walked into the sunroom kitchen where Aliyah was preparing breakfast with the house chef. Although it wasn't required of her, she grew up helping her mom cook meals for the family. And unlike some of her siblings who took issue to hard work it was Aliyah's favorite pastime. As she went about the kitchen, she would be diligent to make sure everything she touched was prepared with love.

While she busied herself cutting fresh fruit, Walid walked up behind her and kissed her on the back of the neck. The chef blushed at their love and Aliyah fought hard to prevent the sensation from stirring up in her panties.

He kissed her favorite spot, the back of the neck, and he knew it.

Walking over to his son who slept in the bassinet next to the open window overlooking the sea, he breathed deeply.

"Where is Morgan?" He yawned and scratched his muscular chest.

Morgan came from America with them, but her advanced age caused her to sleep more than help around the house. But neither Mason nor Banks minded. She supported both the Lou's and the Wales' so long, they would see to it that her dying days would be in peace.

"She made toast earlier. After that she went to bed."

He nodded. "I'm shocked."

"Why do you say that?" She responded by bringing a fresh plate of fruit to the table.

"I'm usually the last one who makes it to the breakfast table. Normally everybody else would be–"

Before he could finish his sentence, the gang piled inside.

First came Blakeslee wearing her new three-quarter inch robe with strawberries throughout. Her hair was tossed up in a messy bun that would unravel with the slightest bump.

Next came 14-year-old Patrick, who was the late Derrick Louisville's and the late Shay Wales' son. Some often felt bad for him because both of his parents were deceased. And with the exception of Ace, Walid and Bolt, he was the only remaining bloodline of Mason Louisville's seed. Patrick was tall and strong. His physical attributes shook Mason when he came upon him to the day because he looked so much like Derrick that it was uncanny.

Next came Bolt Louisville. Mason's youngest son that he shared with the deceased Dasher. Although he took on much of his mother's features, he still possessed bedroom eyes that a lot of the Louisville men carried. Almond colored skin and chiseled muscles was his brand. And he got a kick out of working out with Ace and Walid respectfully in the home gym.

And then came Riot Wales, Spacey's son. He was just as fine as the rest of the gang. He had vanilla colored skin with silky black hair. Although the Wales clan was known for soft hair, his took on the texture of a doll. Had it not been for looking exactly like Spacey, one would have doubted his African American heritage.

Finally, the oldest Wales children came to the table.

First there was Minnesota Wales and her husband Zercy. Although they used to be happy, it was obvious that they had one of their many fights the night before. And since Zercy was private, one could only speculate that although he lived in what could be described literally as Heaven on Earth, he missed the shifty streets of the United States.

Spacey Wales entered next.

He was scratching his belly and stretching his arms due to his sex filled night. As everyone took their places around the table they also looked behind him to see which new female would share breakfast with them today. A lady's man, just cause, he refused to settle down, and loved shocking his family each morning.

Next came Mason.

Scratching his salt and pepper scalp, he strolled into the kitchen and took his place at the end of the table. He may have used the cane these days to move around but it didn't release him from his swag.

Finally, Banks entered.

After all of these years there was something about him that was still alluring. To look at his power, grace and wealth was hypnotic. The man knew who he was and with his billions the world did too.

Morgan entered also, using two canes to take her place. And don't bother mentioning her age or her gait, she would quickly remind you that she had breath left in her body.

Taking his position at the other end of the table, he looked out upon his family. Which meant he was sitting directly across from Mason. Two men sitting at the helm of the table may have confused some. But everybody in the building knew who was boss.

As Aliyah joined her man, and everyone settled down to eat the meal that the chef, with Aliyah's help prepared, Banks noticed the empty seat.

Being together for breakfast was the one requirement that Banks held for the family. He understood that they all had their own minds. But he demanded that every morning he laid eyes on each of them.

Some believed he did this to maintain control. But Mason believed he knew the real answer. In his opinion Banks wanted to ensure that what he willed into existence wasn't a dream. That he had successfully moved his family to paradise.

"Did the band get their meals?" He asked Morgan.

"Yes, sir. They're all set."

He nodded and looked at the empty chair again. "Where is he?"

Everyone looked at the empty space Ace should have taken.

"I'll talk to him, pops." Spacey said.

"There you go trying to control everything again." Minnesota responded.

"I'm confused. How am I controlling things?" He snapped back.

"We have one father." She continued. "We don't need you mixing in."

"Actually, I got two." Walid joked.

Everyone laughed to keep the mood light that they were certain was about to get dark. Besides, after all of these years Spacey never got over his first love. That occurred during the time he and Minnesota were locked in the attic away from the world.

"I'm just saying, if he's not here there must be a reason." Minnesota continued.

"I think he's angry." Blakeslee said, grabbing a piece of bacon and chomping it lightly.

She had Banks' entire face when he was a little girl. Just like Mason did with Patrick, Mason always found himself staring at her, while also being yanked to the past. Through Blakeslee he could finally see the woman Banks would have grown up to be if his heart and desire to be male hadn't changed his fate.

"What would he have to be angry about?" Banks questioned. "He has everything he ever wanted."

"He said, when I talked to him earlier, that you said he had to stay within the walls." Zercy explained.

"Why are you always in Wales business?" Spacey asked his brother-in-law, whom he still despised.

"Listen, when are you going to drop your hate for me? It's been years, man. Let it go." Zercy replied.

"Wait...why do you dislike him so much?" Blakeslee asked her brother, while eating another piece of bacon. "I've been dying to know."

Those who knew cleared their throats and everyone remained silent.

Their history was no place for breakfast or a child.

Walid grabbed a plate and piled it high. Standing up from the table he said, "I'll talk to him, father. Don't worry."

"I'm not," Banks said. "But he should be."

Aliyah rose, grabbed her baby and her plate. "I'll go too."

Before Walid bent the corner Banks said, "Tell him this will be the last time he breaks the rules. Angry or not, I still need to see his face."

Walid nodded and they both walked away.

Ace, Walid and Aliyah sat on Ace's patio and ate breakfast under the magnificent sunrise. They had become so accustomed to paradise that no one really saw it anymore.

What Walid did have however, was a feeling of serenity whenever he was near the ocean. So, in a way that's all that really mattered.

"Anyway, I walked past Blakeslee's room and I heard your father going off." Aliyah said to them both. "I don't know what got into her, but she actually decided that she was going to wear a panty set to the beach."

"Father lost it, Ace." Walid laughed, covering his mouth to prevent food from falling out. "He yelled, *'Everybody sit the fuck down!'* We were all swimming and he was like, *'are those panties?'*"

"Ace let out a light laugh but getting him in a better mood was difficult. Normally the trio would get on well but Ace was still angry about a lot.

He was angry about being confined to the house.

And he also wondered if someone, mainly Walid, was talking behind his back based on what Blakeslee said the night before.

Walid and Aliyah continued to laugh until Walid said, "You had to be there, brother."

Ace nodded. "Let me ask you something, do you think I'm selfish?" He wiped his wild hair out his face.

Walid looked at his girl and then his brother. "Why would you ask me that?"

"I'm still waiting on an answer."

"I think you like things to be your way." He shrugged. "But selfish? I can't see it."

"Blakeslee said that to me yesterday."

Aliyah laughed. "Yeah, right. We both know she idolizes you. And would have never called you selfish."

"She didn't say it like it was coming from her. She made me believe that this was the talk around the house."

"Why you beating yourself up, man? Family talks shit about one another all the time. Who cares where it came from."

"If it's even true," Aliyah added.

"Walid, you don't understand how it is to be me." Ace continued. "Everybody likes you."

"I don't desire to be liked."

"And yet they do anyway. I've even heard pops call me a monster. And he was saying it like it wasn't mad disrespectful. Like I should be happy or something. I'm his fucking son! But he wants me to be you."

Silence.

Walid waved the air, tiring of the sad direction. They just turned eighteen, so Walid was still on his celebratory shit. "Look, we were going to take the boat out. Why don't you come with us?"

"But Banks said—"

"I know what my father said," Walid responded, cutting Aliyah off. "But he'll be fine if he's with me."

The light in Ace's eyes turned on momentarily. "You know what...fuck it! Let's go!"

Ace and Walid were master fishermen. And although they took the boat out on the water to enjoy serenity, Walid took pride in bringing back fresh fish from the ocean that was often prepared over a fire pit by the chef.

With the sun and a cool breeze playing host, the threesome swam in the water and enjoyed conversation about things in the past and hopes for the future. Life felt easy when they were alone. He even enjoyed it when his nephew, who was with them, laughed and played in his arms.

If only he could have what Walid had, Ace reasoned his life would be happier.

Three hours later, tired and hungry, they agreed it was time to return to the shores of Wales Island. But when they saw who was waiting, they wished they'd stayed longer instead.

From the distance they could see Banks standing barefoot on the sand. His hands clasped in front of him. A look of rage on his face. The sun turned his gray accented hair a sparkling silver.

"When we get to the shores let me talk to him." Walid said to them both.

"It's not going to work." Ace responded, never taking his eyes off of his father. "He already has his mind made up. I can see."

"At least let me try, brother." He touched Ace's arm. "Please."

Ace nodded.

The moment the boat was docked Aliyah took the baby and rushed into the mansion. Sand clouds kicked up behind her as she left Banks on the shores with his sons.

Banks' eyes were fixed on Ace. "This is the second time today that you broke my rules."

"Father, it was me." Walid said, stepping between them. "He was sad, and I wanted to take him out. I practically dragged him by–"

"Perhaps if he didn't rape the islander's daughter then he wouldn't be sad." He maintained his penetrating stare at Ace.

"If she said I did anything it was because I was drunk."

"And finally you admit a small portion of the truth."

Walid stepped between them again. "Father, I'm begging you. Don't punish him for what I did. I can–"

Banks shoved him out of the way and stepped closer to Ace. "I have cut off your cards. Frozen your accounts and had your boat and cars relocated. I've also instructed officials on the surrounding islands that if you are seen that you are to be treated like a common criminal. And held up in the prison of their choice."

Walid almost fainted, knowing Ace was about to be livid.

"You will remain in this house until I see a change in you. And if I were you, I would work overtime to convince me that you are worthy of the Wales name."

"So now I'm not a Wales?" Ace said, tears welling up in his eyes.

"Not to me you aren't." With that he stormed away.

CHAPTER FIVE
WALID
"You Owe Me."

"Sir, I have to wash your feet," a house attendant begged as Ace stormed through the corridors after having been stripped of his riches. "Please, sir!"

Wrapped in rage, just that quickly, Ace had broken a third rule. To always wash your feet before entering the house to prevent sand from ending up everywhere that irritated Banks, mainly his room and then his bed.

But Ace couldn't be bothered with the rules.

Nor did he care.

"Brother, you have to calm down," Walid yelled, chasing behind him.

"He thinks I'm a fucking kid!" He screamed, his curly hair flopping over his eyes as the gold *God* chain shined brightly due to the open windows allowing the sun's rays to fall inside. "Well, I'll show him!"

Suddenly Blakeslee rushed toward her brothers. "Ace, are we still going to paint later on to–,"

Ace, blinding mad, shoved the one person to the side that had always been in his corner. She knocked against the wall and struggled to understand what was happening. Her hair toppled from the bun and fell over her face.

Walid, always the rescuer, paused and addressed her eye to eye. Grabbing her softly by the arms he said, "He'll be fine. Go to your room." He wiped her hair away from her eyes.

"But why is he angry? What did father do?"

"Go! Now!"

Confused and bewildered, she ran off crying.

Ace on the other hand disappeared.

On the hunt, Walid finally made it to Ace's room where he stood on the patio. For the moment he wasn't breaking any rules, as Banks said the patio was available to him, as it was encased.

When Walid made it closer, he noticed that Ace was transfixed. He was looking off in the distance and when Walid walked out on the patio, he finally saw what he was staring at.

The band that performed for their party was preparing their plane to leave in the morning. Normally, Banks' plane would be there, but he kept it off the shores so the band could land.

But why was Ace so interested?

"What's wrong?"

Seeing his twin, Ace plopped down and Walid sat across from him. If it wasn't for the gold band pulling his hair back into a ponytail, they would look exactly the same.

"What is it, Ace?" Walid said softly.

It seemed like forever but finally he said, "I'm leaving."

Walid laughed. "Leaving? Yeah 'aight. Where can you go on this island where your father won't be able to find you?"

Ace's eyes fell upon the band again.

"I don't get it."

"You get it. You just don't see."

"But...all I see is the..." Finally, Walid understood and his heart dropped. The thought of losing his brother made him viscerally ill. "You can't do that. They won't let you go with them!"

"You remember the story Spacey told us when he was drunk last year? It was the first time he let us taste whiskey. I hated it and..."

"I loved it," Walid said softly, hoping to change the subject so Ace would stop talking foolishly. "We also caught Blakeslee listening to the story too."

Ace nodded. "That's the night. It was the most wasted Spacey ever got. Even let his girlfriend flash us because we wondered if her titties were real."

"Aliyah's still mad about that shit," Walid admitted.

"Well he told us about how pops hid in the luggage area on a plane to go to an island that father owned. And I think I can do it too."

"You leaving shit out, brother. Because he also said that pops was fucked up. Even to this day he has nightmares about how sick he got flying to one of father's islands."

"But it worked." He scooted his chair closer. "And that's all I give a fuck about."

"But you can't do this!"

Ace sat back. "Don't tell me what I can't do! I'm growing irritated with people trying to control me. Because at the end of the day, he doesn't respect me." He pointed at the door. "He doesn't even...he doesn't even love me. Said I'm not a Wales. You heard him yourself!"

"He was just angry."

"Who says that to their own son?"

"He's just tripping right now, man! If he didn't love you he wouldn't put the press on you the way he does. Let me calm him down and–"

"I made up my mind."

Walid froze.

Whenever Ace said those five words a man could speak to him for hours or days and he would never change his position. Upon that statement, it was official. He was leaving and Walid knew there was nothing he could do about it.

Walid looked down at his hands. "You would do that to me? When you know what you mean to me?"

"Come." He said excitedly, as if it were one of their boyish adventures where they would hide for hours from people in the house as children. "After all, it's your fault father punished me to this extent. You said it yourself."

"I didn't mean that I would do something so–."

"You owe me."

Silence.

Walid rose and looked at the vast ocean. "We haven't been in the states since we were kids." He paced a little. "We don't know that world anymore."

Ace rose too and approached. "We can learn, brother. Together." He smiled. "Come with me! I can't do this without you!"

Walid shook his head. "I...I can't. And if you go, I'll tell father."

Ace took a deep breath. His heart broke in a million pieces. Placing a hand on his shoulder he said, "No you won't." He walked into his room.

WALID

LATER THAT NIGHT

She looked beautiful while she slept.

She looked beautiful all the time to be honest.

But there was something about her sleeping next to their son Baltimore that hit different in Walid's heart. He loved this woman. He would have given the world up for her.

But at the end of the day, he would always choose his brother first.

Every...single...time.

And so, while they slept, he walked over to them and kissed them both on the cheek.

Neither budged.

Neither moved.

And neither would know until the morning that he was gone.

CHAPTER SIX
WALID
"Where is my brother?"

They hit a storm and it was a nightmare.

Worse than either of them could have imagined. Although the luggage area was ventilated and had appropriate air flow due to some people keeping their animals below, it wasn't comfortable or fit for long distance travel. And so they would pay as the cold hard steel of the air appeared to stab into their flesh sending shock waves up their spines.

Originally, they rolled around back and forth in the lower area and they thought if this was the worst, they would survive. But the motion was repetitive with no let up and so Ace had thrown up so much his hair dampened with vomit and tinges of blood.

Walid didn't do much better.

But he managed to keep his bodily functions together. They needed relief. It was he who found an area further toward the back which was high enough for both of them to sit in the corner.

As his brother felt the worst of it, Walid held Ace as he wept due to the discomfort his body was in. Silently, for the moment, they both hated Spacey because had he been a little more sober, a more accurate account of how hellish the experience was would have left his liquored lips.

But it hadn't.

And Walid knew when he returned to Wales Island it wouldn't be that way.

They also realized at that moment how strong Mason was. To have endured the same sensations repeatedly made him appear like a God in their eyes.

And then the turbulence got worse.

RIVER

These days, River was living her best life.

The sun shined down on her tall lanky body that was etched with more black ink than should be allowed. Still, the markings did something for her boyish steeze and her long locs ran down her back, curling at the ends in a bohemian flow. Technically they could be twisted again but the slight bushy-ness made them unique.

River was all kinds of fine.

An entrepreneur who dabbled in street life every now and again, she just placed a down payment on a new shoe store in Baltimore City. It would be her fourth and she had visions of opening more.

It was time to go legal.

Selling drugs was so early eighties.

Although the drug game gave her financial freedom at first, she didn't like the danger that came with dope. She didn't like not being able to trust those around her.

Besides, with Mason gone she didn't have anyone who she felt truly had her back. With the exception of Tinsley who was doing hard time in prison, for a murder she committed, she was alone.

Even if he was home, their relationship had evolved to such a weird place that she couldn't even say he would have her back unconditionally. Besides, he made it clear that he always wanted one thing.

And despite him being a feminine gay man and she being a dominate gay woman, what he wanted was her to be in his life.

She was just about to get in her car when her phone rang. Taking it out of her pocket she glanced down at an unknown number. Curious that maybe it was one of her "*for the moment females*" she answered with a smile on her face.

"What up?"

"River. It's me. I'm calling from a small airport."

She smiled when she heard the voice.

Although she hadn't seen Mason since he left, she spoke to him regularly. Their conversations went on for hours, touching every topic known to man. And when they would talk so long that he would doze off on the phone, it would be Ace who kept her company.

She didn't know she would get so close to the young man everybody thought was trouble, and at the same time it all made sense.

He was Mason's son.

So, to her that meant family.

"What up, lil nigga?" River said excitedly. "Ain't it like midnight there or something?"

"Nah, cause I'm at an airport here."

She laughed, thinking it was play time per usual. "Okay. So, what we gonna do? Get some bitches? Grab some food? What?"

"I'm serious, River. I had to leave. And I need you to come get me."

The phone dropped out of her hand.

Her screen shattered.

The shower played in the background as Walid stood in front of River. They could hear Ace singing as if all was well with the world. In his view he figured it was. After all, he was in Baltimore.

Once again, he got what he wanted.

Walid was wearing a pair of sweatpants and a white T-shirt. Although he was showered, she could still see the residuals of whatever they endured over his skin.

River was stunned.

Number one, to stand in front of either of them would take your breath away. Both young men were so handsome they looked unreal. With their bronzed skin and tatted physiques, she was positive that women would not be able to resist either.

And yet, she wanted them the fuck up out of her house.

She shrugged. "I just don't get it…why did you let him come?"

He ran his fingers through his curly mane and tamed it with a gold hair band, forcing it into a man bun. "I couldn't make him stay. And I couldn't let him come without me. So, here we are."

"Well I have to call Mason. I know you know that."

He glared and moved closer to where she sat on the sofa. "You promised you wouldn't."

"Listen, if Mason finds out you're here and I didn't tell him, that will destroy our bond. That shit ain't fair to me. He's like a father–."

"Like a father ain't the same thing as him being your father."

"That's not fair, Walid."

He sighed and sat next to her. "You're right. But if you tell him without letting me calm Ace down first he'll run. And we will lose him out there. Is that what you want?"

He knew she didn't.

"Just give me some time to get through to him that it's best for us to go home."

She shook her head. "Who leaves fucking paradise for Baltimore City?"

Silence.

"How did you even get here?"

"I don't have the relationship with you that my brother has. But there is one thing that I will never discuss with anybody and that's the trip over here. Let's just say up until we landed, and snuck off the plane, I thought we would die."

She sighed deeply. "So, now what?"

"I'm going to stay with him. Calm him down. And then put a call into Spacey. Have him come pick us up and take us back home. He has his own plane."

"You got it all mapped out huh?"

"You got a better idea?"

Just then, Ace entered the living room with a smile on his face. Loose, wet curls every fucking where. After losing part of his mind about an hour before, it was as if he suddenly forgot what they'd been through on the flight. Rubbing his hands together he said, "Why y'all looking all crazy? It's a celebration! What we doing first?"

"This not no party!" River corrected. "This not no vacation either! You put me in a position by coming here."

Ace bopped to the recliner and flopped down. "You still talking about that shit?"

"You know what, I'm going to the bathroom." Walid said. "I'll be back."

WALID

Walid made an exit for the restroom, mainly to clear his mind. The headache he was experiencing and the heartache he felt having left his girl and son was great.

Unlike Ace, Walid was a family man.

And leaving without an explanation was off brand for him. He only hoped that with time and consistent love, that she would forgive him.

After releasing his bladder and calming down, about ten minutes later he returned to the living room only to see River sitting on the couch with her hands over her face.

But where was Ace?

"What happened? Where is he?" He looked around from where he stood and back at her.

"I'm sorry, man..."

"What happened?" He said firmer.

"He went to the room to get a pair of socks while you were in the bathroom. So, I was about to call Mason. He caught me even though I never got to hit the last digit of Mason's number."

Walid's eyes grew large. "Where's my brother, River?"

"He bounced."

Walid was pissed.

"My pops said he could always trust you. Said you kept your word. I guess that was a lie."

ACE

With nothing of value besides the half million dollar, *I Am God* chain around his neck, Ace strolled the streets of Baltimore City. Even though he was *technically* broke, for some reason hearing the cars and the ambient noise in the background put him at ease. He was confident that with time and a few favors that he would be okay.

At least he hoped.

Walking up to a group of young girls about his age, who were laughing and having a good time at a bus stop, he stood in front of them with his hands in his pockets.

The moment they saw him, their knees grew weak. They were all cute in the face, but he could tell they were exactly what he was looking for.

"What you a model or something?" Red Shirt asked.

"That's what you want me to be? A model?"

"If you asking what I want then we gonna need to go over to the left of that building for privacy." Red Shirt laughed to put on for her friends.

Her three friends giggled in agreement.

"Maybe I'll take you up on it." He nodded. "But look, I lost my wallet and I wanted to know if y'all can give me a few bucks until I–"

"Nigga, please!" Black Jacket spoke up. "You fine or whatever, but I don't know you to be giving you no money."

"Exactly! These Baltimore niggas are the worst."

Fail on his part.

He pushed too hard and would have to readjust his position if he was going to get them to do what he needed.

At the same time, at a very young age Ace learned the art of being conniving. He learned how to get people to do what he wanted, when he wanted. After all, he was in Baltimore due to his skills. And although he didn't have to tap on that skill set on Wales Island, he would need to go back in time and remember his younger days if he wanted to survive.

"You and I both know I'm not from Baltimore," he said calmly.

They quietly agreed.

"See, I was just trying to determine what kind of female you were, and I get it now," he said to Red Shirt, after readjusting his chain. "You want to be with a nigga when it's good, but not help a nigga on the come up."

Her eyes widened. "Yeah whatever."

He tilted his head. "Come on, shawty. Do it look like I need money to you?"

Not only did it look like he had a coin, but it looked like even if he was broke, he could get anybody he wanted to take care of him. In other words, he looked kept.

But it was the *I AM GOD* chain that sealed the deal.

"The thing is, I actually wanted to invite you and your friends out to eat with me and my niggas. But I needed to make sure y'all wasn't no birds first, because my folks got money. They gonna be here in a few hours."

He was wearing Yeezy's and the chain so maybe he wasn't lying after all.

"Do they, do they look like you?" Black Jacket asked.

"Better."

Jaws dropped.

Fifteen minutes later, they were sitting in a restaurant with drinks and food in front of them. Every now and again, Ace would fake like a phone he didn't have in his pocket would ring. This would allow him to be excused from the table and return with a new lie. And due to the alcohol and sweet drinks they were imbibing, their suspicions were down and his game play went up.

While they giggled and talked about all the fun they would have due to the stories he deposited into their minds, he stepped up to the table and said, "They fifteen minutes out. Pay for this shit and they gonna give you the cash when they get here." Ace was speaking directly to Red Shirt.

She looked at him again a bit closer.

There was not a nigga in Baltimore that she could recall that was as put together as he was. He was funny, attractive and had a way of speaking to her that made her believe him. In fact, she needed to believe in something.

So, why not him?

With that, she pulled out her card.

Picking it up, he said, "I'm gonna take it to the waitress so we can bounce when they get here. If my friends come before I return, get the cash and tell them I'll be right back."

He was so firm and confident that she couldn't help but nod several times.

And now, with the credit card in his hand, Ace walked out the door and into the streets.

CHAPTER SEVEN

WALID

"Are you ready to die?"

It looked like rain was coming on as Walid sat in the passenger seat of River's car. They had been looking for Ace for the past two hours and he was beside himself with worry.

It wasn't that he didn't think that Ace would be able to take care of himself. The real reason for his dismay was that he wasn't sure if Baltimore was willing to be forgiving to the damage that he could cause if he couldn't get his way.

"Still mad at me?" She asked looking over at him and then the road.

"I just wanna find my brother." His attention remained on his window for any sign of the man who looked like him.

"I'm confused about a few things."

He looked at her and then turned his head to look back out of the window. "What you talking about?"

"How's it possible to live in paradise and want to escape from it? I know I asked earlier but I really want an answer."

"Shouldn't you be asking Ace?"

"He's not here. So, I figured you would know."

"What I'm saying is I can't answer that for you." He shrugged. "I woke up every day happy to be with my girl and my son. But my brother not feeling it no more."

"Why though?"

He shook his head. "Is this your way of trying to distract me? Because it's not working."

"It ain't about that. I have a bond with Ace. But I don't get to talk to you much. So, I'm just trying to–"

"Read my mind? Get into my head?"

"Kinda."

"I don't spend time thinking about why Ace is not happy. I can't even say I will in the future. All I know is I got to get him back to Wales Island. And I've got to bring him home with me."

"I feel you on that." She nodded, not having much of a choice. "So, when are you going to call Mason? Because you and I both know that this won't end too well once he finds out you both bounced."

"It ain't pops that I'm worried about."

She sat deeper in her seat. "Yeah. It's Banks. It's always Banks."

Ace could tell rain was coming. And although he hit up a few stores and bought some sneakers, sweatpants and T-shirts with the stolen credit card, he didn't have anything that would protect him from the rain.

And to be honest it didn't matter.

He was happy to be away from the strict gaze of Banks. He liked having freedom to do what he chose. Even if at the moment, with the exception of the chain that hung around his neck, he didn't have a cent to his name.

He was still in his head when he saw River pull up alongside him with his brother in the passenger seat. He started to run but already convinced himself that no matter where he went he could hold his own. So in his mind he could entertain them for a few moments with no real threat.

Also he knew that even though she probably called Mason, that it would take at least twenty-four to forty-eight hours for him to make it to the states. Which left plenty of time to get into more trouble.

River's white Benz pulled alongside him and both of them jumped out.

With bags in his hands he raised his arms and said, "I see you found me."

"Ain't shit funny! Fuck is wrong with you?" Walid said, shoving him back once.

A bag fell to the ground and he picked it back up. "Maybe not funny to you but it is to me."

"Why you leave like that?" River questioned, stepping between the brothers. "Do you realize the stress you're putting me under simply by being here?"

"I asked for help and you worried about yourself?" Ace questioned.

"You didn't ask for help. You took it, little nigga!"

"Listen, I'm not going back to the island. You can take it how you want, but if you're trying to convince me to do that, you won't. My mind is made up."

There were those words again.

Ace could tell that they were angry, but he truly didn't care. He was going to do what he desired and let everybody sort it out. If he didn't, what was the point of escaping the island?

He came too far.

Not only did he feel well within his right to live his best life, but he knew he was an adult now. He wasn't a kid. And that meant anything that happened to him he had to agree to, including going back to the island.

They were back in the car and cruising down the road. Walid in the front seat. Ace in the back.

Every now and again, as they passed various stores and fronts, Ace would think about what life would be like if he was a full resident. If he could be amongst the people who had the same heart as he did.

He was still in his head when he saw a beautiful chocolate girl, with fine light brown hair running down her back, posted at a storefront. She was wearing a yellow top and light blue jeans which were ripped at the thighs and knees. Her body was literally shaped like a coke bottle, and she put Ace on pause.

He readjusted his dick just to calm down because she was that cold.

The women in Belize ain't have shit on the native of Baltimore.

She was locking a beauty supply store which had yet to be open and slipped into a silver Tesla.

When River reached a light and was waiting on it to turn green, once again Ace poured himself into the city streets, leaving her car door hanging open.

"Fuck is you doing now?" River asked, speaking mostly to herself.

When the girl turned on the engine, and propped in her driver's seat, Ace slipped inside the passenger's seat and said, "Thanks for waiting. I'm ready."

Her eyes widened with fear but his beauty knocked down her guards. At the end of the day, she unarmed herself momentarily for a monster.

"What are you doing in my car?" She yelled, whipping her hair behind her ear. "Get out!"

"You my Uber, right?"

"Uber?" She frowned. "Are you fucking serious?"

"Yeah, I ordered an Uber and I thought you were it." He smiled and looked ahead. "Let's go."

Again, she didn't feel fear but it didn't mean she was comfortable with the way he was applying pressure either.

"I don't know if this some kind of weird pick-up line, but I'm not available! And if you want to live the rest of your days, I suggest you never talk to me again."

He grinned. "What if I tell you I'm not gonna do that?"

"Are you ready to die?"

Just then the passenger door was snatched open and he was yanked out by River.

"Fuck is you doing now?" River said, shoving him with two flat palms away from the girl's car.

Unbothered, Ace maintained a smile on his face as he continued to look at the beauty in the Tesla. River was the least of his worries. "The answer to your question is yes!" He said to the beauty. "I'm ready to die, if it means getting to know you!"

She smiled and hated herself for falling for his charms.

"Sorry 'bout that, shawty," River said to the girl before closing her door. "Enjoy the rest of your day."

She sped off, looking at him once more from the rearview mirror before disappearing from the scene.

River led a laughing Ace back to the car where Walid sat shaking his head in the front. Before she pulled off she said, "Y'all can get mad all you want, but if I'm gonna do this, I'ma need help."

She sped off, almost hitting the car in front of her.

CHAPTER EIGHT
JOEY WALES
"60 days."

As Joey sat in the chair in his dining room with his beautiful wife Sidney riding his dick, he looked up at her piercing blue eyes. Although many years passed, they still managed to make love four times a week.

And although Joey was inclined because he enjoyed the way his wife's pussy felt, he knew her real reason for wanting to be so consistent was because after so many years, she still couldn't get pregnant.

Gripping her by the waist and sucking on her pink nipple, he pushed into her once more. Unlike the other fuck ceremonies that were for pleasure, this push went deeper because he wanted her to finally fulfill her dream of being a mother.

Within seconds, he filled her with his cream as he kissed her passionately. Without releasing pressure, he maintained his shove for a moment, realizing that for her, every drop was important if he was going to have a Wales heir.

When they were done, she cried.

Pushing her back softly he said, "What is it?"

She got up, grabbed her pink silk robe and wrapped it around her body. Wiping her blond hair out of her face she said, "Nothing."

He slipped into his boxers on the floor and flopped next to her. "I need you to stop saying nothing and talk to me."

"Don't speak to me in that way, Joey."

He threw his arms up. "In what way? Why does everything have to be so serious with you? Tell me what's on your mind."

"I want a child. And I–."

"Why is this always a thing, Sydney? We have a life." He looked at their large home with vaulted ceilings and crystal chandeliers. "We have each other. What the fuck is your thing with needing a baby too–."

"I want an extension of you. I want a bigger experience for you. And I will never have that, unless I have a baby."

He stood up, walked away and returned. "Maybe if you stopped sucking on them fucking sleeping pills you wouldn't be in this predicament."

"Wow..."

He knew he went too far but now rage was in charge so she could suck his dick for all he cared. "What I want to know is this...are you telling me, after all this time, if you don't have a baby with me you can't be happy?"

She sniffled. "I never–."

"Answer the fucking question?"

"I...I don't know! Alright? I don't fucking know!"

He hung his head and dragged a hand down his face. "You know, I never said this to you, but I feel the need to say it now. Had I known you would be this miserable I would have left."

Slowly she rose. "Do you mean...you would have–."

"Went with my family. To Wales Island."

"So, it's my fault you decided to stay?"

"Who else?"

She held her barren belly and ran off. Her feet slapped against the hardwood floors until the door slammed shut.

In his mind, as he often did, he imagined his little brothers playing on the beach. He reasoned Banks would be happy too, and probably wrestling with Mason even though they were older.

Instead, he was in the Baltimore County area, arguing with Sydney.

Joey would've never pressed things so hard, but she backed him in the corner and he was done with the stupid shit. There was another reason he refused to bite his tongue. His deep-seated fear was that if he wasn't careful, he could be nudged back into the heroin addiction that once took over his life.

"I could've been happy on that island and here I am arguing about a kid that I don't even want. Fuck her. If she wants too–."

DING DONG.

Frowning, he walked over to the alarm console and looked at the small security camera. He wasn't expecting company. In fact, he never had company. So, when he saw River and two men who looked like larger versions of his little brothers, he stumbled.

Them ain't the niggas he saw in his daydreams that was for sure.

Grabbing his dark velvet blue robe in the closet, he rushed to the door and pulled it open.

Just their presence, took his breath away.

Joey, River, Walid and Ace were sitting on the enclosed patio watching the rain pour down over his massive lawn. As he bore witness to the story they just talked about how they escaped in the cargo area of a plane, he found himself filled with rage.

They had it all and gave it up for nothing, in his opinion.

And then he took in their newfound bodies.

When they left they were boys who were nowhere near men. And now they stood before him like Greek Gods. With their bronzed skin, gold-tinged curly hair and tattoos, they resembled lighter versions of the people from Solomon Island.

"Both of you niggas stupid," He said, as the rain grew louder.

River nodded in total agreement.

"With all that shit y'all just said, I still don't understand what would make you leave paradise to come back here. We ain't out here doing shit!"

"It ain't for you to understand," Ace said.

"You see, that's where you wrong." He pointed at him. "You a Wales, so it is for me to fucking understand."

"You know what, I'm sick of having to explain why the fuck I wanted to do what I wanted to do. I'm grown." Ace said firmly.

"And yet, here you are looking for me to help you find your way."

"What I'm looking for is support from family."

"You had that on Wales Island." He pointed outside.

"Nah, I had control. You don't know how it is to have father quarterback your every move. To have a play in everybody you deal with and everything said."

He sounded like a fool.

Joey *did* understand.

As he sat on his patio chair, he had vivid memories of Banks controlling their bodies, actions and who they dealt with. In fact, Banks still controlled a lot of his moves. Banks just didn't think he knew.

It was the Wales way!

"All I wanna know is why you here?" Joey said plainly. "Because I'm not about to tell you what you want to hear."

"I brought them." River interrupted. "They ain't wanna come."

He threw his hands up. "I'm waiting on the why."

"Because they your brothers. And if something happened to them, I would ruin the relationship with the one man I consider "real" family. And I can't have that. So, I came here so I wouldn't be the only one who knew where they were."

"I brought you some tea," Sydney said, carrying a tea kettle on a beautiful sterling tray with cups, cream and sugar.

Although she was being helpful, she also wanted to look at the men the twins had become. And it was Ace who's eyes rested upon hers.

And she, upon him.

"Thanks, ma'am," Walid nodded.

"You got anything stronger?" Ace asked. "Cause this ain't–."

"Nigga, I'ma need you to focus," Joey said clapping his hands together. Looking at his wife he said, "You ain't have to do that. We good."

"I did it because I wanted to." She stomped away, slamming the patio door in the process.

Ace, sensing her need for attention, placed a closed fist on his mouth and laughed heavily. "Oh, oh, now I see why you mad. You beefing with–."

"60 days," Joey said to him, interrupting the fun and games.

"What you talking about?" Ace frowned.

"I don't know why you came, but you have 60 days to figure it out. Not a day more."

"What you gonna do if I stay longer?" Ace said as he tilted his head. He rose and stepped closer to show he was both taller, stronger and younger than his brother.

Joey laughed and remained seated.

Unmoved.

"Fuck is funny?" Ace questioned.

"You so dumb, you think a few muscles make you invulnerable. You in America little brother. Out here, it only makes you fall harder to your grave."

"Fuck you just say to me?"

Joey rose. "Sit the fuck down before I drop you."

There was fire in Joey's eyes and Ace reclaimed his seat.

"Thank you," Walid said. "60 days should be enough. And we appreciate it too."

"Good. And I got a few other rules also."

Ace threw his hands up in the air. "Now what?"

"You staying here...with me." Thunder clapped the sky. "And you gotta tell me everywhere you rolling in advance."

"You know what, it's whatever, father." Ace said sarcastically. "But you still ain't answer my question."

"I stopped listening to you an hour ago. So, how 'bout you tell me again."

"What happens if I don't do what you want? Father couldn't control me. What makes you think you can?"

"Test me. And then you'll find out."

CHAPTER NINE
MINNESOTA WALES
"I don't see this ending too well."

Minnesota was in her yoga room practicing her downward facing dog. After many attempts to get pregnant while also trying to prevent Zercy who always seemed grumpy from breaking her mood, yoga was the only thing that helped.

But it was difficult these days.

Zercy was once so positive and lately, as the years went on, he seemed distant and cold. The sudden change had her thinking that something dark was about to happen. Which was something she hadn't felt in ages.

She was just about to change positions, when Blakeslee rushed into the room, causing her to topple to the floor.

"Sorry, Minnie!"

"What did I tell you about calling me that?" She got up, grabbed a towel on her bench and dabbed the sweat away from her yellow skin.

"I'm sorry, Minnesota!" She said, rolling her eyes. "But something is wrong."

"What you going on about now?"

"I think Ace is gone!"

She frowned. "You know, at some point you're going to have to let whatever that thing is you have for him go." She pointed in her face.

"I don't understand."

"He's your brother."

"I know that." She said, lowering her head. "So, why can't I be concerned about my brother?"

Minnesota shifted a little. For a moment she realized that it was possible that she was reflecting her own experiences about her and Spacey's volatile past onto her little sister. "Just tell me what makes you so upset."

"Earlier today I heard Aliyah crying in her room." She was so close now she could smell the milk on her breath. "When I walked in and asked her what was wrong, she slammed the door in my face."

Minnesota shrugged and sat down. "So?"

"So, I think Ace ran away and Walid ran after him."

"Ran where?" Minnesota stepped back.

Blakeslee stepped closer. "Somewhere on the other islands! I'm not sure. But we have to find out before father finds out and makes Ace's punishment deeper."

"If Ace ran off and Walid followed him, they deserve everything they got coming." She shook her head. "If they knew how good they got it here, they would be kissing his feet."

"Please, Minnesota. I need help. I have a feeling I'm right."

Minnesota sighed and said, "You know what, just come with me."

Spacey was getting head in his room by Trisha, a woman he saw every now and again who had hopes of being an official fixture in the Wales mansion.

He was just about to bust when someone knocked on the door.

"Fuck," he said to himself. "Go away!" He yelled at whoever was about to mess up his flow. And then looking down at the female he said, "Don't stop. Drink every drop."

She had no intentions on ceasing. Instead, she sucked and sucked until his cream rolled down her throat and into her stomach.

When done, he pulled her up and looked into her eyes. "How come I feel like whenever you do that, you love it?"

She kissed his lips. "You know what I want."

"What's that?"

"For you to finally choose me. You do that and I will fall asleep with your dick in my mouth every night." Easing out of bed, she slipped on her yellow spandex dress. The imprint of her nipples were present, which made him wonder why she wore clothes at all because she looked naked. "Hopefully you'll eventually give me what I deserve." She walked toward the door.

"Where you going?" He asked. "Ain't you trying to eat breakfast?"

She looked under the door at the two sets of feet waiting. "You have company and I'll see you later." She winked and pulled the door open.

Minnesota and Blakeslee were on the other side. Giving her that, *you a nasty bitch look*.

"Ladies," Trisha said before walking in between them and down the corridor.

Minnesota rolled her eyes while Blakeslee rushed inside.

Seeing his sister coming his way, Spacey pulled the sheets up over his body and said, "Wait, I'm not dressed."

Blakeslee didn't care. Unlike many of the older Wales members, youth and getting what she wanted taught her zero boundaries.

"He's gone! He's gone!" Blakeslee yelled, giving the very shortened version.

Minnesota walked in and leaned against the wall. Looking at Spacey she said, "You know, one of these days your dick is going to fall off."

"What I do with my dick is no longer your problem."

"Wait...it was her problem before?" Blakeslee responded looking at her sibs.

Neither Spacey nor Minnesota wanted to speak of things before her time.

"Who's gone?" Spacey said, returning all back to the topic at hand.

"Ace!" Blakeslee said.

"Okay..." He shrugged. "Well maybe he'll come back after he gets out of his mood. If he don't get locked up."

"He's not in a mood." Blakeslee sniffled. "He's seriously upset. And in an hour we will be forced to go to breakfast and try to explain why he isn't there to father."

"She's right." Minnesota said. "Between the three of us we better come up with an answer to tell pops. Because I don't see this ending too well. For none of us."

CHAPTER TEN

RIVER

"I need some money."

River stood in front of her floor-to-ceiling window overlooking Baltimore City. Although she'd seen the same view many times, it never got old. In fact, when she had moments of stress, looking out the window was the only thing that brought her relief.

"What do you want me to do?" She said into her new cell phone, which she replaced after shattering the screen of the other one.

"I want you to be happy that I'm coming home." Tinsley said.

"I never said I wasn't. I bought you a car. Put a down payment on your new crib and everything." She walked to the center of her floor.

"New crib? I thought I was staying there."

"I never said that, Tinsley."

"Something has changed. What's the real issue?" He asked. "And don't try to brush me off because I'm getting agitated."

"You are not my boss."

"River, over the past few days you've been absent. I'm not saying I want your life to revolve around me, but I do want a place in your heart. I mean why you acting different? Before I was coming home you put on that me getting out was the best thing that ever happened to you. And now–."

She flopped on the sofa. "Do you really want to know my issue?"

"Yes."

"I don't want you thinking that you and I being an item is what's on my agenda. I've been dating and–"

Tinsley laughed.

She glared. "Fuck is so funny?"

"Whenever you're forced to reflect on what you want, you bring up a bitch. When that's not going to change anything." He laughed harder. "Not for me anyway."

She glared.

"Look, I'll be home in less than a month. Whatever you got going on you have to make time for me."

"Why do I have to?"

"You and I both know why. I mean, do you really want me to say that over the phone?"

She didn't.

Tinsley was in prison for a crime River committed.

Many years ago, after believing Tinsley's boyfriend meant to do Tinsley harm, River decided to take his life in Tinsley's apartment. The thing was, Tinsley never knew. A few things happened and after a while they found some evidence to support that Tinsley may be involved in the crime.

After all, the DNA was found all over his place.

So, when Tinsley was eventually arrested, he selflessly took the beef. Wanting nothing more than for River to be there when it was all said and done.

It was a high price to pay for her love but he did it willingly.

"Tinsley, can we talk about it when..."

There was a knock at the door. River was literally saved.

"River...are you–."

"Tinsley, I have to go. Just call me back. Somebody's at the door."

Ending the call abruptly, from where she sat she yelled, "Who dat?!"

When no one answered, she walked carefully to the door, with her hand hovering over her waist that held her weapon. On the other side were Ace and Walid's muscle-built asses.

She was annoyed.

This whole situation coupled with Tinsley coming home had her stressed beyond belief. The last thing she needed was the twins in the mix.

Reluctantly, she opened the door and walked away. They entered without an invitation just like they did with her life.

"Now what?" River asked, flopping on the sofa.

"I need some money." Ace said.

"So, get it from Joey." She shrugged. "I know for a fact Banks blesses his account every month."

"He won't give us any." Walid responded. "Said our broke asses shouldn't have left in the first place."

"What do you want with money anyway?"

Ace stepped closer. "The way I see it is like this. The better time I have the more I'll be able to say it's worth it and leave everybody alone. Ain't that what you want?"

"Stop with the sales pitch and get to the point."

"I just need some money to hold me over. Are you going to give it to me, or do I have to start robbing niggas?"

Walid took one step back and dragged a hand down his face.

"You not bold enough to do that." She said assuredly. "This Baltimore!"

"You wanna test me?" He grinned, wild curls covering his sinister eyes.

CHAPTER ELEVEN
WALID
"He went to New York."

As Walid and Ace sat in the back of an Uber, his mind floated on to Aliyah and his son Baltimore. Over the past forty-eight hours Ace had consumed every moment. Always wanting to know how he felt and what he was thinking about being in their hometown.

While some may have thought that proved that Ace had a good side, and that maybe he wasn't as selfish as some believed, Walid knew Ace's need to have answers to this question was his way of living the experience fully. Because taking the adventure alone was one thing, but experiencing the adventure through Walid also, would justify the escape.

But what no one knew, with the exception of Walid, was that many years ago he was able to secure cell phones from an islander back home. Although he didn't foresee having to use the phone ever, just like Banks he thought a few steps ahead. It was important to be able to stay in contact with wifey in the event they were separated. At the end of the day, the phone in his possession was meant for him and

Aliyah to communicate if he ever returned to the States.

In a sense, he always realized that his brother would never be happy. He always predicted that he would want to go back to where he was born. Paradise was too slow for his twin.

And what could be faster than Murdermore?

They just passed a large seedy motel which boasted hourly rates when Ace said, "What you thinking about?"

What he was thinking about was the moment he would have separation from him so he could call his wife on the secret cell phone. But what he said was, "What do you want to happen with all of this shit?"

"I don't get it."

Walid looked out the window and back at him. "You wanted to come for a reason. And I don't want you having any excuse, when it's time for us to go back home, that you didn't complete the task."

"Always with the past."

"What do you want to happen here? Because I'm going to do everything in my power to help."

Now he was talking.

Ace rubbed his soft palms together. "Just admit, brother, that you are as excited about all of this as I am."

"But I'm not. I got a wife and–"

"Yeah, yeah, yeah." He waved the air as if saving himself from pesky mosquitoes. "You have a wife and kid. I get all that."

"If you really got it I wouldn't be here."

"Listen, I know you got Aliyah. You make it known on a repeated basis. But I'm trying to have-."

"Ace, I'm not fucking around! I need to know right now what's the plan. Because whatever it is, we need to do that and hit it back home."

"Y'all good back there?" The driver asked from the rearview mirror. His question was more for himself than his passengers. Because pretty or not, if he had to dump them on the side of the road, he was fully prepared to do so.

"We good." Ace smirked. "You good up there?"

The driver rolled his eyes and continued to steer the car.

"What do you want?" Walid questioned a bit softer.

Looking at him square in the eyes he said, "What you got."

"Everything I have you could've had. With no problem. So, stop talking about you want-."

"I'm talking about the life, Walid. I want the wife. The kid. Everything."

"We went through this already. And any female back home would have loved to be with you. Asked to meet you and everything. And they would have stayed–."

"Stayed with me just because we billionaires."

The driver looked at them again, as if studying their faces for the future.

"Nah, I remember the one chick who used to hang out with Trisha liked you a lot. You just didn't like her because you said she asked too many questions. But guess what, that's what females do when they feeling you."

"Her questions felt different though. Like she was trying to get the code to make me want her even more."

"Ace, I think you making excuses."

"Do you remember that old movie pops and father like? The one where the dude lives in Africa and came here to get a woman?"

"Coming To America," The driver blurted. "But he didn't come here. He went to New York. So y'all in the wrong city."

They both glared at him and he refocused on the road.

"That's how I feel," Ace whispered to his brother. "I won't know if whoever I meet wants me unless they don't know me. Unless they don't know about father's fortunes."

Walid gazed at the *I AM GOD* chain dripped around his neck. "So, that's why you wearing that chain." He grabbed his wrist. "And this bracelet with–."

"I'm never taking this off." He snatched away. "Blakeslee gave it to me. Because she's the only one who understands me." He lifted the gold and diamond pendant. "And I'm never taking this off because it reminds me of who I am."

"So I don't know you, nigga? Blakeslee is really the only one?"

"You know what I mean."

"The chain is a bit much." Walid continued. "Because the way you sound, without it you ain't shit."

"You asked me what I want. It's simple. I want everything. Starting with the girl at the shop."

"You mean the one in the Tesla?"

Silence.

"But how do you know she's not taken, Ace?"

He melted into the seat. "When have I ever let that stop me?"

Walid shifted a little. "Look, if you gonna do this..."

"If *we* gonna do this."

"If *we* gonna do this, then you can't move like you've been moving. Everything gotta be different.

That means yanking females, walking into people's houses without knocking and taking what you want...is off the table."

Ace laughed.

"I'm serious!" Walid pressed. "All that rich shit you do on the island can get you killed out here. It can get us killed."

Ace thought about his words. "Okay."

"I'm serious, man. If I feel like you don't get what I'm saying, then I'm done. And I'm going back home with or without you."

Ace nodded. The thought of his brother leaving now was too much. Besides, with him at his side, he felt it doubled his power.

"Okay."

Walid sighed. "You gotta listen to me. You gotta understand everything I'm saying. Or this won't work."

"I promise, man." He raised his hand in the air as if he were a patriot. "I'm all in."

Walid breathed in and breathed out so hard he felt weak. "Then everything you want, as long as I'm here, will be yours."

Ace grinned, readjusted his chain and smiled.

CHAPTER TWELVE
ACE

"You can't expect me to change overnight."

The mall was crowded as Ace and Walid thumbed through racks to pick up the perfect gear. River, in an attempt to get them up out of her face gave them five thousand a piece. To be honest the money was lightweight to her, but for Walid's plan it would be just the right amount of day cash.

Ace, however, had other ideas on the clothing he would need to get the girl.

When Ace scooped up a flashy designer shirt, Walid snatched it away. "Why you keep picking up that loud shit?"

Ace looked at the shirt and didn't see the problem. "Because I like it."

"It ain't about you liking it. It's about sticking with the plan. Nothing that will say wealth." He looked around at all the gaudy colored clothing. "Or hood rich."

After being shot down, Ace continued to look for gear that he felt would appease himself and his brother. But after hours of searching, he still came up short. Irritated, he walked out of the store and flopped on a bench in the mall.

Walid followed.

"What's wrong?" Walid asked.

A group of girls almost fell down the escalators looking at the men.

"Is this a set-up?" He asked.

"What you talking about?"

"Wally, you say you want to help me, but I feel it's different." He shoved a few disobedient curls from his eyes.

"I would never set you up." He paused. "You sound crazy."

He smirked. "Yeah, alright."

Walid frowned. "What's that supposed to mean?"

"What about when we were eleven-years-old? And you were with your friends on the island. Everybody thought it was funny to do the cinnamon experiment. You wouldn't do it but you had me do it instead."

Walid laughed. "That was a joke."

"But I choked. Almost couldn't breathe."

"I didn't know you felt a way about it. And so what, people laughed at you."

"It wasn't that *people* laughed at me. It was that *you* laughed at me." Ace went deep.

Walid looked at the girls who were staring at them so hard, he wondered if they could hear his private conversation.

When Ace saw his brother's attention redirected, he got up, and said, "Get the fuck up out our faces for I smack the shit out of you."

The girls ran away crying.

"You see what I'm talking about?" Walid said, when he returned to his seat. "That shit gonna get you killed."

"You can't expect me to change overnight."

"Fair enough." He sighed. "But look…if I knew you had a problem with that cinnamon shit, or that your feelings were hurt, I would have never done that. You're my brother. And if I tell you I'm going to help you that's what I mean."

"I need you to be serious."

He placed a hand on his heart. "I am."

"Even though our other brothers may try to turn you against me, you can never let that happen."

"I won't."

"Promise me, Wally."

"I will never let anybody fuck with our bond."

Ace took a deep breath. With his brother on his side he really felt he couldn't lose. "Okay so what's the plan again?"

"You have to pick clothes to make it look like you don't have money. Simple items. It's bad enough you wear the chain. But you gonna have to tuck that in your shirt too."

"So, basically you want me to wear muted shit like you?"

"Exactly. Because I know what you don't. The clothes don't make me. I make them. And at the end of the day it's the only way to see if this girl is feeling you or something she thinks you can do for her."

Ace knew he was right but the idea of not looking as shiny as he felt on the inside rubbed him the wrong way. At the same time he was fully aware that if he wanted the girl he would have to listen to Walid.

And so, he *planned* to do just that.

Wearing muted gear but still looking fresh as ever, Ace leaned up against the wall beside the mystery woman's beauty supply store. He had yet to get her name, but he felt that was just a part of his check off list that he would inevitably accomplish.

Besides, her name didn't matter if at the end of the day he wasn't able to get her heart.

Within fifteen minutes she pulled up and parked in front of her shop. The moment she saw him she shook her head, grabbed her purse and exited her car. The sun bounced against her beautiful chocolate skin causing her to shimmer. And her real silky brown hair blew in the wind.

"You're late," he said.

"Am I going to have to call the police?" She asked as she removed her keys from her pocket and entered her shop. Ironically enough, she left the door open and he entered too.

"Why would you do that to your future?"

She laughed loudly. "Yeah, okay."

He frowned. "What's funny?"

"Tell me something and I want you to be honest."

"I'm listening."

"Do those tired ass lines work on other women?"

Ace knew she would be a challenge but on no planet did he think a female would come at him so hard. More than anything he was embarrassed. "It's not a line."

She tossed her black Hermes purse on the counter and turned around to face him.

Ace smiled when he caught her looking him up and down. He'd seen that gaze before and could tell that even though she put on as if she wasn't interested, that she was definitely feeling him.

He wanted to whip out his chain on the bitch.

"Let me make this clear so we won't have any problems in the future." She pointed at herself. "I'm not available. Not now. Not in the future. Not ever."

He shrugged. "I know you're not available."

"Meaning?"

"How you going to be available if you're taken? By me."

Just then he could hear noise in the background of her shop.

It appeared to catch her off guard too because she turned around immediately and rushed in the direction of the noise. Past the empty shelves and supplies. As he followed and looked at the mess everywhere, it was obvious that there was a long way to go before the shop would be open for business.

Pulling a door toward the far back, Ace saw six men banging with hammers and putting more shelves up. Despite the work they were clearly doing, she didn't seem too pleased.

"Miss Arbella, we didn't know you would be here this early." Worker Number One responded. "We would have come out and spoken."

So, Arbella is her name? Ace thought. *Ace and Arbella. That sounds about right.*

"Why wouldn't I be here? It's my shop."

"It's just that we wanted to get a little further ahead of schedule so we can meet your deadline a bit sooner."

Ace walked closer to the men and looked around. She was so mad that she didn't seem to notice him.

"First off, you already missed my deadline. So that's not the issue." She slapped the back of her hand in the palm of the other. "The issue is that you didn't get my authorization first. At this point I feel like you're spending my money without me asking."

Just then, more workers piled inside from the back door. She shook her head and dragged her hand down her face.

"Listen, we're sorry ma'am." Worker Number One responded. "But we don't plan to be here long."

"At this point just make it quick. And just so you know I'm not paying for more hours. This whole thing should have been done last week."

"Sure." Worker Number One frowned.

Ace walked up to her. "You good?"

"Listen please don't come back here. I don't want anything to happen to you."

"Why do you keep saying something will happen to me?" He asked.

"I can tell you're not from around here." She wiped her long hair out of her face. "Because if you were, you would already know. My boyfriend is dangerous. And I'll leave it at that." She shook her head and walked away.

Instead of disappearing and heeding her warning, Ace looked at the workers. There were so many of them putting up shelving it was hard to see the plan.

Some were painting. Some were banging and it all looked a mess.

Ace had never done a hard day's work in his life.

No scratch that.

Ace had never done *any* work in his life.

But that didn't stop him from grabbing a brush and a can of paint and going to work. From where he was posted, he briefly saw Arbella looking at her cell phone. There appeared to be a look of frustration and sadness on her face.

It was okay though.

He had plans to make every day bright if she played the game right.

Of course, he had rules.

There were things he needed his girl to do if she was going to be with him.

But all of those details would come later. Right now nothing mattered more than etching himself in her world. In a way that would leave an imprint.

An hour later she returned to the back to see him laughing with a few of the workers. She didn't know what shocked her most. The fact that the majority of the work was done, or the fact that he was still there.

Rushing inside with wide beautiful, angry eyes, she grabbed him by the hand and pulled him toward the front of the shop. The white specks of paint on his hands added to the appeal.

Before she touched him he was only mostly sure that she was the one. But after she touched his hand, and he felt "that thing", he was one hundred percent certain that she would be his wife.

"First off, what is your name so I can tell the police when the time is right?"

He chuckled. "Ace."

"Okay, Ace, why are you still here?"

"What you mean? I was working." He pointed in the back with his thumb

"But I didn't ask you to do that."

"You shouldn't have to ask your man to help. But I was working and making sure that the issue you had with the contractors would be a non-factor."

"What issue?"

"Am I tripping? Because earlier you said they were moving slow on the job. So, I saw to it that the work got done today." He shrugged. "What part of this don't you get?"

"You are going to–."

"Look, the fellas will be done in an hour. I'll be back soon. That way I can help you put products on the shelves and you can open for business. You shouldn't have to do this on your own. You said you got a man right?"

"I do."

"Then where is the nigga?"

Silence.

"I'll be back in a few days."

"A few days?" She frowned.

"You want me to come back sooner?"

"I wasn't saying that. I–."

"I'll check on you later. Until then, stay stress free. I don't need my wife getting ugly in the face. It's one of my rules."

"Rules?"

He winked and walked out the door.

LANCE LAURENT

The sun beamed on the shiny black Maybach across the street from the unopened beauty shop. And yet it didn't do anything to brighten the mood of the man inside.

A descendant from Nigeria, Lance was the youngest child in the Laurent dynasty and he felt entitled to the power that generated before he was even born.

The Laurent's were well established real estate moguls of their own right. The only person who had more money than them, who was born from that area, was Banks Wales. Due to his smart business decisions and his late grandmother's knowledge in the haircare industry.

As Lance sat in the passenger seat of his car, with his henchman who moonlighted as his assistant in the driver's seat, he glared at the curly headed exotic man leaving the shop.

Who was he?

And more importantly, what did he want with his beautiful Arbella Valentine?

Grabbing his cell phone, he dialed her number for the twelfth time that day. And like the previous calls, this one went unanswered too.

Was the stranger the reason?

Just like his tycoon father, Satchel Laurent, he would not be ignored.

And so, after the tenth call, her voice bled through his phone in irritation. "What do you want, Lance?"

He shifted a little. "How long are you going to stay mad at me?"

"It's not about staying mad at you. I'm just tired of you trying to control me. I'm tired of you trying to control my body. You don't get to–."

"I need the answer to my earlier question, Arbella. And I need you to give it to me now."

"And I already told you, what I do with my body is my business."

"Are you pregnant with my child? And if so, are you trying to get rid of it just to hurt me?"

"Wait...you...you had me followed?" She yelled. "Again?"

Silence.

"Listen to me, Lance. And I'll try to talk slower so you'll understand. I never want to hear from you again! It's over!"

When he saw his cell phone screen go dark, he lit it again with another call.

This caller only allowed the phone to ring once, respecting the Laurent name.

"I think she's going to leave me." Lance said.

"Nonsense." He chuckled. "My daughter loves you. She would never–."

"Mr. Valentine, I saw someone leave her shop. And I need to know who he is."

"I'm sure your father can get right on top of–."

"He's growing irritated with Arbella not wanting to commit, sir. So, I need you to check for me."

He sighed. "Understood. Do you have a picture?"

He looked over at Nelson and nodded. Nelson, without a word, grabbed his phone and sent the picture that was captured earlier when Ace's curly headed ass bopped out of the store.

"You should have it now." He informed.

"I got it. But don't do anything. You know she's easily nudged."

"I want the dream, Mr. V., of the Laurent's and Valentines combining wealth. But I need your daughter to make it happen. I need her to love me. To submit to me."

"Your dreams align with mine. And we both will have what we desire. Just give me a little more time."

CHAPTER THIRTEEN
THE WALES'
"Trouble always seems to follow us."

The ocean waves put on for the Wales clan on the outside, as they sat inside their breakfast sunroom.

But it didn't matter.

Once again Banks was sitting at a table that not only excluded Ace, but also Walid, Aliyah and Baltimore.

Mason, sitting at the far end, readjusted to the left a little. "Before you get mad you have to understand that they are grown men. And you–."

"Mason, don't tell me not to be angry." He sipped his coffee. "I've earned the right to every one of my emotions."

"That's your problem." Mason buttered his toast.

"What's my problem?"

"You have created an environment where can't nobody tell you anything."

"You seem to do alright speaking up for yourself," he glared.

"Because I've also earned the right." Mason paused. "If the boy is gone then maybe we should give him his space while he–"

"I've given him everything."

Mason rolled his eyes, and everyone readjusted in their seats.

Even Morgan who was still a wealth of wisdom despite age taking its course sighed deeply. At the end of the day all those present knew that the two friends were about to be at odds.

The only question was if they fought, how long would it last? Because the earth could crumble and Banks and Mason would always be.

"It's one thing to give everything," Mason said. "But it's another thing to keep throwing it in everybody's faces."

"When do I throw it in anybody's face?"

Everyone looked down. And Banks caught their motions.

"Pops, everything is going to be fine," Spacey said, clearing his throat. "Ace ran off on the island because he's–"

"Spoiled! Just like everyone of you!"

"That's not fair, dad." Minnesota said. "Why you mad at us?"

"Isn't it though? Because I've done all I could to give you children what I didn't have. And I'm rewarded like I did something wrong."

"And again you misread the point." Mason said. "If the boy is feeling uneasy about anything, maybe listening to him could have made the difference. But you chose otherwise. And I'm trying to understand why?"

Everyone looked at Banks, hoping he would have an answer they could all accept. But it was obvious if he did, he wasn't willing to share.

"Pops, I really can bring him back," Spacey said. "Just let me talk to them alone."

"I'll give you some time. But after that I'm getting involved."

"You always do," Mason responded.

Baltimore Wales played happily in his playpen as Aliyah sat on the floor next to him whispering to Walid on the phone in secret. It was the first time since the whole ordeal started that she was able to get some relief.

She had finally heard from her man.

To say she loved him was an understatement.

He literally was her prince charming.

Before Walid, she lived in an environment so violent and filled with rage, that it took its toll on her physically. Her autoimmune system kicked up in weird ways that even if she could have afforded a doctor no one would have been able to help her.

It wasn't just about her outward circumstances changing with him in her life.

Walid really saw her.

He catered to her emotions. Cared about her thoughts. Concerned himself with her well-being and swept her off her feet before convincing Banks to allow her to live in their home.

He agreed.

Banks may have been set in his ways, but one of his great qualities was that he loved being surrounded by people. Besides, he literally had the wealth to care for anyone who needed a helping hand. And Aliyah was no different.

Two months into their dating, suddenly the autoimmune system issues which plagued her for so long disappeared.

She was happier.

Thriving.

All under his love.

"I care about Ace too," Aliyah whispered. "You know that. But you leaving your family was the wrong move. And so unlike you, Walid."

"He's my brother."

"Why is that always the justification? It's almost as if he's your alter ego that you enjoy losing yourself into every now and again."

"Baby, don't do this."

"Do what? Put a mirror in front of you so you can see your own shit?" She swiped the tears away. "You left us. And you promised never to do that, Walid."

"I'm coming back to you. I promise. I just have to let Ace work through what he has to work through before returning. It won't be forever. Just–"

Suddenly her bedroom door flew open.

This was odd as they usually knocked before entering. She reasoned with Walid gone that her privacy went with it. And since she wasn't supposed to have a cell phone, she tucked it quickly behind her back as she bore witness to Spacey, Zercy, Blakeslee, and Minnesota entering her room.

"Whatever happened to knocking?" Aliyah responded, as suddenly she felt uncomfortable sitting on the floor.

Spacey stood in front of her and looked down. "Why weren't you at breakfast?"

"I didn't feel like eating."

"Ever since you moved into this mansion you've helped the chef prepare our morning meals. And now that's changed?"

"Spacey, you have plenty of slaves around here. You don't need me."

"That's not fair." Blakeslee said, pointing down at her.

"Is it? Or is it tough hearing the truth?"

"Where is he?" Spacey said, stepping closer.

"I don't know."

Minnesota stepped up too. "You're lying. Now where is he?"

"Where are *they*?" Spacey corrected.

Suddenly Aliyah looked down and cried hard. It was a cry so painful her entire body jolted. She was concerned that if she didn't get herself together the auto-immune issue she once had would return. Wreaking havoc on her life and her ability to take care of her son.

"He's going to be sooooo mad at me." She sniffled.

Spacey reduced his height and sat across from her on the floor. "Aliyah, you don't know the history of this family. But there is a story that seems to follow us wherever we go."

Blakeslee, always interested in the past but never getting answers, stepped closer to hear his every word.

"I don't understand." Aliyah said.

“Trouble always seems to follow us. And when trouble comes, death is next. So, I need to make sure my brothers are safe.”

“Please, Aliyah.” Blakeslee said, now being scared more than ever. “Help us find Ace.”

“And Walid too,” Minnesota responded.

“I didn’t mean it that way.” Blakeslee told the room. “It’s just that we all know Walid can take care of himself.” She shrugged.

“Aliyah,” Spacey said, returning her attention back to him. “Where are they? On Shepherds Island? Coates Island? Pearl? Where?”

She shook her head softly from left to right.

“Aliyah, please say something,” Zercy said. Since he normally didn’t speak on family matters, this shook her gently.

“America.” She whispered.

Spacey fell backward.

Minnesota dropped to the bed and Blakeslee fainted.

“What...what are you talking about? How is that possible?”

Zercy tended to Blakeslee, bringing her back to the present. It’s a good thing too because the other siblings didn’t seem to care that the child hit the floor.

“They hid in the cargo area of the band’s plane.”

Spacey was so overcome with fear that it was a struggle to keep himself from vomiting. This was exactly the mixture needed to throw their family out of whack.

For a moment they all looked at Spacey.

Waiting for the words they hoped would come next.

"I'll go get them."

Relief washed over them like a warm shower.

"I'm coming with you," Minnesota said.

"Me too." Zercy responded.

"Okay. But none of us, not one..." He looked at Blakeslee. "Can tell pops."

"Done." She nodded her head slowly.

Focusing back on Aliyah he said, "Now give me that phone you hiding behind your back. I may need it later."

CHAPTER FOURTEEN
WALID
"Time got away from us."

Walid and Ace were walking toward their brother Joey's house after a long night in Baltimore. Although after talking to Aliyah and the phone call ended abruptly, which made him upset, he actually enjoyed himself in the city. This shocked Walid because up until that point he assumed it was his brother that needed the adventure. But now he was thinking that maybe, just maybe, he needed the moment too.

"I'm telling you, Walid, I think I got her already." His curly hair bounced with every step.

"Take it easy though." He touched his chest with the back of his hand. "We don't want to jump the gun. Remember the plan is to get her and bring her back to the island. But if she got a dude–"

"I don't care nothing about that, nigga."

"Here we go again."

"How you sound?"

"That's your problem, Ace. You don't ever look at the full picture. You too young and dumb to know the real world."

"The full picture? I was the one that spent hours with father going over his businesses. While you spent your time kicking it with pops and picking out the best whiskey that hit the market."

Walid thought about what he said.

Although Ace and Banks disagreed, when it came to business ventures, they were close. Banks enjoyed Ace taking an interest in his life.

While Walid continued to have a quiet bond with Mason that lasted a lifetime.

"You know what, I never thought about it." Walid started. "It seems like you got a better relationship with father when things are going good but it's pops that always has your back when you get into trouble."

"I know. That is crazy. Why do you think you're so close with pops?"

"I can't call it." Walid sighed. "I remember being a kid and being strongly connected to him. In ways I couldn't really explain."

"Maybe you don't gotta explain." Ace continued as they approached Joey's door. "Maybe all you got to do is–"

The statement was cut short when both of them were yanked inside the house. Not by Joey or River who was standing there, but by two beefy strangers who weighed about 750 pounds respectively.

One of them, named Push, was also young and eager to prove himself.

"Bring them to the back." Joey said, walking away.

Not even a minute later, they were sitting on Joey's patio. The sky was deep purple with golden stars flickering above. The two beefy strangers stood on the right and left of the twins, who were seated on a bench.

While River was propped next to Joey.

"I thought I told y'all niggas to let me know what's going on at all times." Joey said, leaning forward.

"Sorry, Joey, man." Walid said. "Time got away from us."

"That's just it. Time can't get away from you out here. This not paradise. This nothing like what y'all are accustomed to."

"You act like we ain't from here." Ace snapped.

"Your mentality ain't." Joey said, knocking his own temples once.

"Tell them the truth, man." River said calmly.

Joey looked at her seriously.

"They need to know if they going to be moving in these streets, who they *really* are."

Walid leaned closer. "What's going on?"

"You may know our father as a shrewd businessman. But we came up on dope money."

Ace looked at Walid and busted out laughing.

Joey, visibly irritated, sat back and dragged a hand down his face. "What's funny, Wig?"

"You expect us to believe that father deals in dope money?" Ace asked.

"Not anymore. But in the beginning that was the family business. It wasn't just him. It was me. Minnesota. Spacey. Your brother Harris that you never got a chance to meet. Mason...all of us. That was our way of life."

Walid was stunned.

But Ace suddenly looked at life a bit differently. Finding out he came from such dark circumstances made his chest swell a bit more with pride.

"How much money are we talking?" Ace asked.

"More than you could count if you died one hundred times and came back a hundred more."

"Why are you telling us this now?" Walid questioned.

"Taking Ace from that children's home all those years ago wasn't the only reason the island was created. There are people that are looking to make their come up off of a Wales seed. Kidnap. Extortion. Whatever. We equate to dollars."

"Or a Lou too for that matter." River added. "Which both of you are."

"And if you don't watch the holes that you crawl into, you may bring trouble on yourselves. And our family once again."

Joey was just about to go deeper when his cell phone rang. When he saw the number on the screen he sat back in his seat and sighed.

Showing the screen to River first and then the twins he said, "I don't recognize this number."

Walid did.

It was Aliyah's cell.

"But since only a few people know my number, it means they know you're here." Joey continued.

"How you know that?" Ace shrugged. "It could be anybody."

Walid knew it wasn't anybody. Why would his girl be calling Joey, whom she knew only in name, if it wasn't his family back home?

"It's somebody on the island. I know it." Joey persisted.

River leaned forward, elbows stabbing in her knees and yelled, "Fuck!"

Spacey tucked Aliyah's phone back into his pocket as he stood in front of his black Escalade which was kept off Wales Island. Since the only way to reach the island was by boat, which all of the Wales' and Lou's had.

"He didn't answer," Spacey said, looking at Minnesota and Zercy.

"We gotta go get them." Minnesota shrugged. "Because they are there. I feel it."

Spacey took a deep breath and walked to the hanger which housed his plane. The moment they entered, a man who had been exposed to so much sun, his skin looked like aged leather, stepped in front of them. He wore a stiff suit and smelled of liquor.

"Ahhh, Mr. Wales. How can I help you?"

"I need my plane."

He frowned. "Your father didn't tell me you'd be flying out today."

"What difference does it make?" Zercy asked. "We need the door lifted and the craft gassed up."

"Well, if Mr. Banks won't give me the okay, I–."

"It's my plane! And I want it now!"

"No problem. No problem." He said, raising his hands. "This can all be settled quickly. Let me talk to Banks and I–"

This irritated Spacey because he kept that plane in the air. In fact, one of his ways to flex for the ladies was by taking them on a trip through the blue skies.

He knew Ace's trouble had officially trickled down to him.

"Don't call him." Spacey warned.

"Sir, why don't you want me to call him?"

"Just open the garage and let me at my vehicle."

"And I said I won't be able to do that." He laughed once.

It was Zercy who struck first.

A fist to the nose.

The man was so put off that he almost forgot where he was. To make sure he knew they were serious, Zercy hit him again. He continued to strike him until the man realized Banks was the least of his troubles in that moment.

"Now, where is the plane?"

With blood pooling out of his orifices, he pointed, "In the back. We will gas it up and raise the door."

"Good, and for future reference, stay the fuck out of Wales business," Spacey responded.

Zercy rubbed his knuckles upon hearing Spacey's favorite comment. In his opinion nobody wanted to be in their messy ass business in the first place.

Thirty minutes later, after paying the man at the counter enough money to change his life, to prevent him from allowing leather face to call his father, Spacey, Zercy and Minnesota were cruising.

As Minnesota sat next to him in the co-pilot's position, she smiled at the way he handled the skies.

"What you grinning for?" Spacey asked as Zercy sat comfortably on the plane drinking whiskey.

"Women eat this shit up don't they?"

"Every time," he admitted.

She sighed. "You know, this is the one thing I wish I had allowed dad to teach me."

"I didn't know you were interested."

"I never saw the reason to learn how to fly. And now, in my opinion, being able to go anywhere you want, when you want, is real freedom."

KNOCK. KNOCK. KNOCK.

The banging below almost caused Spacey to fumble the controls. "What the fuck is that?" His heart thumped with fear.

Slowly, Zercy and Minnesota moved toward the hatch. What they saw consumed them with anger.

It was Blakeslee Wales.

Which meant she would be the fourth Wales member to flee paradise.

"Fuck!" Spacey and Minnesota said at the same time.

Ace left with River, to go to her house, the night after learning about descending from dope money. He prodded her with so many questions about the past that he ended up staying the night.

At first, Walid thought it was odd that he would leave him at Joey's alone. But after being unable to get a hold of Aliyah, he wasn't in the mood to go anywhere.

Sitting in the living room of her penthouse, River and Ace were laughing and enjoying one another's company as they always did, when suddenly River felt unusually sleepy. It was the kind of exhaustion that could only come from drugs.

Confused, when she looked over at him, he wore a smile on his face. "Wait, what you put in my drink?"

"One of Sydney's sleeping pills."

"But...but why?" Her body slumped over sideways on her couch, as she stared at him sitting in the recliner.

"If it's true that they're on the way, I need some time alone. To get at my future wife."

When she finally dozed off, he grabbed a few more stacks of cash from her stash.

With fifteen thousand in his pocket he snatched Tinsley's car keys to his new white Tesla and rushed to the garage. After pressing the button on the keypad a million times, it finally answered to its name with a chirp.

"There you go." He grinned, running toward it.

Slipping into the butter pecan-colored seats, he turned the engine on and it was so silent he almost felt it didn't start. But when he put it in drive, it proved ready to roll.

After learning that his family was possibly on the way, he knew time was of the essence. Walid's plan had to be canned in lieu of speed, if he was going to get Arbella.

He needed space.

He needed to be alone.

He needed to be himself.

CHAPTER FIFTEEN
ARBELLA VALENTINE

"Everything. And still it won't be enough."

The library in Mr. Valentine's penthouse was massive and it was Arbella's favorite place to spend time with her father. Although they shared many things together, it was their love for reading that made her visits regular.

For days and weeks on end they would immerse themselves into books with the sci-fi theme, often to the point of believing things to be real. Laughter and heavy theories combined with real life events would keep them hostage for hours, as they delved deeper into their make-believe worlds.

After finishing the final chapter, she closed the burgundy hardback book and said, "I didn't want it to end."

He sat the book on the side table and picked up his vodka. "Me either, sweetheart." He took a deep breath and a deeper sip, before looking over at his beautiful daughter. "But how are you?"

"Wow..." She sat deeper into the designer highchair.

"What?"

"You normally want to talk about the book a bit longer before we get into pleasantries." She giggled. "I thought for sure you would have an opinion on Sir Allen. And how what he experienced matches the experience the actor just went through. When he went missing for five years, only to return–."

"Claiming someone took his memory," he recalled, finishing her sentence.

"Yes, so what changed, father?"

He smiled. "I see you know me too well."

"What's wrong, dad?"

"I'm worried about you."

She frowned. "Why do you say that?"

"Arbella..."

"Dad..."

Space filled the massive room and finally, as if a light was flicked on, she understood what was happening. "He called you, didn't he?"

"Sweetheart."

"Why do you allow him to do this to our bond?" She wiped thick strands of her naturally silky straight hair out of her face.

"No one could ever destroy our bond." He spoke. His skin was dark, and his head was bald. And yet there sat thick rows of black and gray eyebrows over his eyes.

DING DONG.

Her eyes widened and she shook her head slowly. "You told him I was here too?"

"Just talk to him, sweetheart. He loves you."

"I won't be forced to be with someone I don't want. I won't make the mistake mom did."

He glared. "Be easy with me. I am still your father."

"I'm starting to wonder if I should call Lance daddy instead."

"Maybe you should. Because your disrespectful ways are part of the reason you and Lance have so many problems. Don't end up like your mother."

She hated him.

Within a few more seconds, Lance entered after the maid allowed him inside.

When Lance Laurent entered a room, you knew he was confident. His African heritage was connected with the motherland, and height resembled that of a basketball player.

With Arbella being no more than 5'6 if she was an inch, her frame was towered by his 6'4 inch one.

Lance walked in quickly, shook Mr. Valentine's hand and then shuffled up to Arbella with his hands behind his back.

"I'll leave you two alone." Mr. Valentine responded. But when he went to kiss Arbella on the cheek, she turned away. "Very well." He walked out, leaving his daughter and Lance alone.

Once the door was closed, Lance said, "Sit down, Arbella."

"I don't want to."

"Do you want me to get loud?"

Slowly she took her seat. "What do you want with me?"

"Everything. And still it won't be enough."

"Lance...what do you want?"

He took a deep breath, and she could tell he was forcing himself to say something he didn't believe. "Look...it's like this...I'm sorry."

"For what this time?"

"If I'm not mistaken we are still in a relationship. And I should treat you like a partner, not like someone who has committed a foul."

"I'm not one of your business transactions. You can't control or monitor me."

The look he gave her let her know that's not what he felt. "Listen, you may be angry but you owe me an–."

"I don't owe you anything."

"That's where you're wrong. It was me that bankrolled your beauty stores. It was me who paid for your new car."

"I had money."

"All of the money your father makes right now is dirty. More than anything the government is still watching all he does. Because we both know, if he goes back to prison, it will be forever. So, he needs me and my family to clean it up through our properties and–."

"I don't give a fuck about any of that shit! All I want to know is, what does that have to do with me?"

"Who was the dude who left your store? With the curly hair?"

Her eyes widened. "So, you're having me watched?"

"Let's just assume I am watching everything you do. Now who is he?"

"I don't know him."

"So, why did I see you talking to him in your shop?"

"He's just some stranger who wandered in and got in the way. He's harmless enough."

"The thing is, I'm not."

"I know. And I told him."

"So, you had a conversation with this stranger?"

She cleared her throat. "Like I said, I don't know him. And this is not about him. It's about you and me."

He glared and sat in her father's chair. Dusting invisible fibers off his shirt he said, "Did you do it?"

"I'm not talking about it, Lance."

He stood up and propped himself in front of her. "Did you get rid of my baby?"

When she moved to leave, he yanked her by the arm and dragged her over to a trash can. "What are you doing?"

He removed a kit from the back of his pants. "Take this."

Her eyes widened and it took her a moment but, in the end, she was staring at a pregnancy test. "Lance...I..."

"Take it now!"

"So, you want me to pee on this, in my father's library?"

"I'm still wondering why I've given you a direct order, and you haven't complied."

Trembling, she tried to reconcile with what was happening. But she was also no fool. She remembered the last time she saw this look in his eyes. He had beaten her so badly that she spent two weeks in the hospital.

When she regained consciousness, directly after the event, she called her father for help and support. She figured that if she told him what he'd done, he would stop pressing her to be with him and finally realize she was not in love. Instead, every time she tried to tell him where she was, he would cut her off.

It was obvious that her father was not interested in playing the hero.

She was so embarrassed at his weakness, that she eventually said she was going out of town for two weeks. Knowing that this would be a chance for her to heal the wounds Lance inflicted.

Pushing down her pants and then her panties, before long a pad was revealed. He knew then that she definitely aborted their baby, because it was not her time to be menstruating.

Yes, he knew her menstruation schedule as if it were his own.

"You will pay for this, Arbella."

She pulled her clothing up.

"You will pay, I promise you." With that he ran out the door.

CHAPTER SIXTEEN

ACE

"Do you accept the challenge or not?"

The moon was high, and Ace had been sitting down the street from Arbella's beauty store for hours. He saw construction workers come and leave due to not being able to access the premises and he felt in his spirit that something was wrong.

Yet, he knew she would return.

And he was right.

When he finally saw her it was well past eight and she looked distraught that he didn't go in directly behind her, as he originally planned. He wanted to be a part of the solution, not the problem. Instead, he allowed her to enter her store so she could calm down first.

He noticed she kept the lights out as she busied herself inside. Twenty minutes later, she departed but didn't return to her car. Instead, she walked a few places down to a bar.

Everything in his body wanted to rush inside. Instead, he asked himself, what would Walid do? And so, he stayed patient.

Fifteen minutes later, he exited the Tesla and entered too.

ARBELLA

Tito's bar and grill was halfway packed with joyful customers.

It was owned by three nephews who were taking care of their sick uncle and had become a staple in Baltimore. After hearing their story in the paper, locals worked overtime to ensure the business stayed afloat. Not only did they accomplish their feat, but the business was better than ever.

This was one of the reasons Arbella enjoyed the restaurant so much. In her mind they represented what family should be. Not what she was going through now with her father.

She was sitting at the bar on her phone when suddenly someone slipped next to her. When she turned her head to the right, she was happy to see Ace. And if she was being honest, relieved. It didn't mean that she was going to let him know. After all, he was borderline stalking.

Instead of speaking to him, she looked at him briefly and focused back on the phone in her hand. She realized at that moment she didn't have anyone to text. After all, she had since abandoned all of her friends for her dream and Lance, leaving her virtually alone.

When she saw something on the bar out of the corner of her eyes she shook her head when she noticed what was written upon it. There were vertical and horizontal lines drawn on a napkin. And in the middle sat a circle.

Ace had started a game of Tic-tac-toe and was waiting for her move.

Sighing deeply, she snatched the pen from his hand and drew an X.

He took the pen back and drew a circle.

On and on they went until Arbella won the first round.

While this game continued, there was not a word being said between the two. Ace didn't hit her with any of his witty banter. And she didn't bother to tell him why she wanted him to leave her alone.

Instead, they shared each other's company, game after game, in silence.

After the score was tied, he chose to speak first. "Okay let's raise the stakes." He smiled, wiping his hair from his face.

She tucked her hair behind her ear, trying to prevent from falling for his charms. "I liked you better when you were silent."

"No you didn't." He winked.

He was right.

"I'm listening." She sighed.

"Whoever loses this round has to take a shot." He rubbed his hands together and she looked at them. It was obvious that he never did a day's work in his life.

"Are you even old enough to drink shots?"

"Are you?"

"Actually, I'll be twenty-one next year." She bragged.

"So, basically no."

She laughed and he smiled.

His looks unarmed her again and yet she wasn't a fool. She knew quite well that there was something dark lurking behind those fine eyes and she wondered why she sensed similarities between him and Lance.

"Okay. You have a deal." She said.

And so, the next game got serious but in the end Ace won.

Not to be considered a loser she yelled, "Double or nothing!"

"Oh you going that hard?"

"Do you accept the challenge or not?" She shoved him lightly.

He liked the way it felt. And wondered what he could say to get her to touch him again. "I've never run away from a challenge in my life."

She giggled. "That's the first thing you said since I met you that I actually believe."

And so the next game began. X's and O's marked up the napkin. They were so intense, that people around them stared in anticipation. Patrons of the bar didn't know what was more exciting to watch. The game. Or the fact that there was something brewing between the two.

I mean keep it real.

They looked fucking good together.

Like they were made for each other.

When it was all said and done, it was Ace who came across as the winner. And so as she took her four shots, she looked at him with slits in her eyes. "This was a setup, wasn't it? You're really good at this aren't you?" She wiped her mouth with the back of her hand and sat the shot glass on the table.

"And so are you."

"Nah. You're a master. If there's such a thing as being a master in Tic-tac-toe."

"You can be a master at anything if you give it enough focus." He sipped his whiskey on the bar.

Just like his fathers, he was starting to like the taste. "But yeah, I played before. I'm sure no more than anybody else."

"But I still feel like you've been holding back."

"Okay let me stop doing that." Suddenly he leaned closer. Not close enough to kiss her but close enough to let her know that whatever he was about to say was real. "I like you and I feel like you made for me. And I know you've probably heard that before but I don't give a fuck. Because with me it's true."

"I get the impression that even if I did hear it before, you wouldn't care."

"At the same time I feel like time is of the essence, Arbella. So, if we gonna see if this can work, we gotta do it now."

She frowned. "If you think I'm going to have sex with you while you go back to your island, think again."

He leaned backwards.

He never told her he was from an island.

Immediately his thoughts went back to what Joey and River said. That the world knew he was a Wales. And that because he didn't know the enemy that made him an open mark.

"I never told you I lived on an island."

"I didn't say you lived on an island. But look at your skin. You don't get a tan that perfect unless you live away from here. Florida or something."

He was relieved.

And she was confused.

She nodded. "You said time is of the essence. So, what do you want from me, Ace? Because I'm at a point where I can't play a lot of games. I don't want anybody coming into my life with motives. All I want is to be."

"To be?"

She sighed deeply. "You ever move about the world and feel like there are people forcing you to do, say and act as they wanted?"

Of course he did. It was the reason he left Wales Island to begin with. "I got an idea what you mean."

"So, I'm telling you that I need you to be honest. What do you want with me?"

He took a deep breath. "Over the next couple of days I want you to give me a chance."

"A chance to what?"

"A chance to show you that if I'm not mistaken you could be the one. To do this we gotta bypass the getting to know each other stage. I don't have time for it. I need your extreme focus on me."

"Wow."

"If my plan doesn't work, which means you'll be mine, then I'll never bother you again. And I promise, you will never see me again either."

"But you don't even—."

"You're the one, Arbella. I feel that shit."

"You can say that after only meeting somebody for a couple of days?"

"Yeah. I believe you can."

She thought about her life.

Her father clearly wanted her to be with Lance for reasons that involved finances. She wanted to believe her father loved her but the more he pressed the issue about her being with him, the more she believed Lance wasn't the one.

And although she couldn't say who this Ace character was, having met him recently, she wondered if maybe she could give him a chance.

Maybe if she tried just a little harder he could be her escape.

If only for a moment in time.

CHAPTER SEVENTEEN
WALID

"We have less than 48 hours."

The wind whipped around Joey's estate as he looked at River and Walid. Their moods were different but the irritation was unified. Ace had done whatever he wanted per usual, to get at the mystery woman.

"I'm just not understanding why he drugged me," she said as she stood up and looked down at Joey and Walid as they sat in the living room. "This nigga put some shit in my drink! I mean is he serious?" She paced the floor rapidly.

"I feel you, I do, but I don't know that that makes any difference right now." Joey responded.

She stopped walking. "*Don't make any difference right now?* One minute I'm kicking it with him and the next he putting something in my drink and that shit cool with you? One of your wife's pills at that."

"Don't get mad at me!" Joey yelled. "I been told you not to trust his ass. Ace been this way since he was a kid." He pointed at her. "You're the one who should have been smarter."

"Excuse me?"

"Stop!" Walid yelled standing up.

They gave him the moment.

"No matter what happened, at this point we have to think clearly and find my brother. Because whatever he's doing is not only making a problem for himself, but other people too."

River knew shit was serious. But she still felt a type of way. "I'm just not understanding why he would do it like this. If the little nigga wanted the car, I would have given him the keys."

"Because he's scared. When he gets like this he thinks his family is against him." Walid explained. "It's just a matter of time before father comes. So, he's trying to move quickly before that happens. But if I know my brother, shit is about to get worse first."

"Exactly. So, we have to find him instead of staring into each other's brown eyes!" Joey interjected. "The last thing I need is pop's getting mad at me too."

Joey and the older Wales children called Banks pops. While the younger generation referred to Mason as pops and Banks as father.

"I think I may know where he is." Walid said calmly.

They both looked at Walid.

"Then tell us!" Joey yelled.

Before anything else could be discussed, suddenly there was a knock at the door. Joey gave both of them knowing looks.

Walking towards the sound he didn't bother glancing at his security camera. River and Walid followed.

Opening the door he was surprised to see Spacey, Minnesota, Zercy and Blakeslee on the other side.

Both Joey and River were yanked by Blakeslee's beauty. To say she was stunning was an understatement. What the fuck were they eating on that island?

Greek God and Goddess juice?

The last time they saw her she was in diapers. Now she was in stretch pants and halter tops. Her body filling out in ways that didn't give a man a chance to remember she was only fifteen.

"Are they here?" Spacey said getting right to the topic.

Suddenly Walid pushed forward and his question was answered.

He sighed in relief. At least the trip wasn't for nothing.

"Pops doesn't know you're here yet." Spacey said.

They all took a deep breath.

Walid dragged two hands down his face.

River leaned against the wall as if the weight of the world was lifted.

And Joey placed two hands on his hips and paced a little.

For now, they had more time.

"I figure we have less than 48 hours before he realizes we aren't on the surrounding islands and that we're in the states." Spacey took a deeper breath and looked at the twin. "Basically what I'm saying is, you niggas gotta come home."

"Ace is missing." Joey responded. "And we don't know where he is."

"Y'all dropped the fucking ball already?" Spacey yelled.

CHAPTER EIGHTEEN

ALIYAH

"Do you like it here?"

When Aliyah walked into the lounge and saw Banks and Mason sitting quietly by the fireplace her heart throbbed. In her arms was her son Baltimore Wales and she almost dropped his heavy ass on the floor, she was so scared.

As the fireplace crackled, and cast a glow on his seed, Banks said, "He's perfect."

Mason, who also shared the boy's bloodline said, "Facts."

"Thank you." Aliyah muttered.

"Bring him to me."

Slowly Aliyah walked over her baby and placed him in Banks' waiting arms. He playfully cooed and looked up at his grandfather as if he was fully aware of the secrets he held.

"Sit down." Mason told her.

As Banks kissed Baltimore's hand, he said, "We don't get a chance to talk much. He sighed. "And to be honest that's our fault not yours."

"It's okay, sir. I know you're both busy."

"No excuse. I should make time for family, because family is important. Has always been and will always be to me."

She tried to get comfortable in her seat but suddenly it felt as if she were sinking. Deeper.

Deeper.

Deeper.

When she readjusted to the right and then the left, nothing provided her with comfort. And so she decided to sit stiffly in the middle and wait for whatever was coming next.

"Do you like it here?" Mason asked while he sipped whiskey. "I'm talking about here...on Wales Island."

Placing a hand over her heart she said,"I absolutely love it here. Your family saved my life."

"Saved you?" Banks repeated. "Do you *really* mean that?"

"Of course I do, sir."

"Then why didn't you come to me the moment my sons left this island?" Banks rose and placed the baby in her arms.

However, in the moment she felt too weak to hold her own child.

"Because...because he went after Ace." She looked up at him. "And I thought he would be right back."

"In less than 48 hours Ace, Walid, Blakeslee, Zercy, Spacey and Minnesota have all left. And even now they haven't returned." Banks remained standing over her. "If you know something, it is very important that you tell me now."

"I have to pee."

"Now." Banks said.

Suddenly tears trailed down her cheeks and dropped on the baby's forehead. She shook her head rapidly from left to right.

"Stop! We don't have time for your fucking games!" Mason yelled from across the room. "We're going to ask you this and we're only going to ask once. So think carefully before lying to us. Where's our family?"

What was happening now had been rehearsed briefly over her last conversation with Walid. He said there would come a time when his fathers would question her about their whereabouts.

He said that they may threaten her.

Isolate her.

And even throw her out.

But no matter what, the moment he returned he would save her again just as long as she didn't tell them that he left Wales Island.

Up until that moment the plan was to be strong. Besides, she had all faith that Walid would do his best when he returned. And yet there was no mistaking that Walid wasn't the next or even the third person in charge.

So, if she was going to hold back information, she had better be fucking sure she was prepared to lose it all.

“He's in America.”

Banks almost fell.

He didn't know what he expected her to say but he definitely didn't expect to hear those words. Perhaps he was on Pearl. Or Majorca.

But not America!

He figured the worst that could happen was that his children were trying to get ahold of Ace. And break him out of his temper tantrum yet again.

But this was the worst-case scenario.

Did his children actually flee paradise?

He and Mason zipped out of the room as she cried harshly, startling the baby in her arms.

CHAPTER NINETEEN
ACE

"I'll drive."

The cool air caressed their faces as Ace and Arbella exited the bar. Her car was a few stores up and the Tesla he snatched was a bit further back.

"Well, I had a good time," she said standing in front of him.

He wrapped an arm around her lower back, tugged and looked down at her pretty face. "Me too." She hugged him tighter and moved to walk away, when he grabbed her hand and said, "I don't want the night to end."

She shrugged. "Me either. But...but..."

"Say what's on your mind."

"I'm not ready to have sex with you."

He shook his head. "The last thing I'm thinking about is sex. I just want to roll somewhere for a while. I don't care where we are."

She smiled, exposing her perfect teeth. "I know a place."

"Then what we waiting on?"

Fifteen minutes later they were sitting on top of a high skyscraper, on the roof. The moment he walked out and took in the magnificence, he stumbled a bit. He had never seen anything more perfect.

"How did you get access to this building?" His head moved slowly from left to right trying to take it all in.

"Is that the question you really want to ask me right now?" She giggled.

Ace continued to look down at buildings that were so tall it made him realize how high up they really were. Don't get things strange. He had become accustomed to beauty.

Every day he awakened on Wales Island, he would be seduced by golden sand and aqua colored water. Skies so brilliantly blue that they looked as if they were tinted. But in his opinion nothing was more impressive than seeing buildings lit up in an array of different lights and colors.

She took his hand and led him over to a group of chairs. He sat in one and she sat next to him. Neither taking their eyes off of the scene.

Ace was feeling the place, he truly was. But he needed to know was this her thing? To bring niggas up the top in an effort to impress. If it was, he would have remained. But he would've definitely treated her differently.

"I got to know. Who's your man? And your father?"

She sighed. "Out of respect, I will never, ever tell you who they are. And if they ever asked me about you, the same will be true. I've seen the things that happen in the darkness and I don't want anybody hurt."

"I have a right to know."

"Do you though?" She responded. "Because to be honest, I just met you."

He sighed. "Okay, well how did you get access up here?"

"This building is owned by my father. It was sold to him for $1,000."

He frowned. Not believing such foolishness. "I don't deal in real estate, but I know enough to know that this building is worth way more."

"It is. The money was for the paper."

"I'm confused."

"For the contract so that anybody looking at the paper trail could see an official sale was made. But the real price to buy this building was me."

He glared. "Are you telling me that your father sold you to someone?"

"I'm always uncomfortable when it comes to talking about my father."

Ace understood. "I'm not going to press you if you don't want to reveal."

"It's not that. It's just that lately I'm starting to believe that every action that we had together has an ulterior motive."

"You mean you and your father?"

She nodded. "When my mother was injured many years ago, and went into a coma, it was just my father and me for a while. And even those times were fleeting because he was in and out of prison for different drug charges. But those moments where we were alone were the most important moments in my life."

Ace nodded and continued to look out ahead. Not wanting to look her square on, for fear she wouldn't be able to complete her story.

"But now I'm sure that I don't mean anything to him."

"I don't believe that." Was all he could say.

"I like you, Ace. And these past couple of days you have kept me entertained. But when I tell you my father is as he is, you must believe me. You don't know what it's like to have a rich dad who wants nothing but to control you."

Of course, he knew what it meant.

As they spoke, he was certain that Banks was taking to the skies to pull him away from what he was starting to love.

Baltimore.

But instead of responding and sharing his story just yet he said, "My bad. I'm listening."

She looked down at her pink manicured nails and back at him. "I lied about not wanting to be with you tonight."

Now he looked her directly in the eyes. "What you saying, girl?"

"Take me somewhere."

"Where?"

"To be honest, I don't even give a fuck."

When Ace pulled up at a cheap motel suddenly Arbella changed her mind about not caring about their whereabouts.

Although she was willing to be with him for the night, she still had taste. There were certain places she wouldn't be caught dead in and the Fourteen Motel which charged by the hour was one of them.

At the same time Ace was without identification. So, he needed to go to a place that would allow him to pay in cash and not ask questions.

When they stepped out the car and looked up at the trashy building, she walked up to him and said, "On second thought, I know a better place."

He was relieved.

"Come with me. I'll drive."

The Four Seasons was the perfect place.

Arbella had rented a suite, overlooking Baltimore and now they stood in front of it, towels wrapped around their bodies looking at one another. The gold bracelet Blakeslee gave him remained on his wrist, and the chain on his chest was finally revealed.

She looked at the brilliance of the diamonds, "God huh?"

"Who else?" He spoke.

The lights were out, but neither cared because the city lights illuminated the frames of their bodies just right.

Staring down at her, he tucked a strand of hair behind her ear. "I feel like I painted your fine ass for me."

She smiled. "Yeah 'aight."

"I'm dead serious."

"I have to tell you something."

"Listening."

She looked out of the window and back at him. "I faked a pregnancy. And then I faked losing it too."

"Why?"

"At first my ex said he didn't want children. So I told him I was pregnant hoping he would leave me alone. Turns out he wanted kids with me after all. So I faked an abortion."

"Magnificent lies just to be free?"

"I'm sorry. And I understand if you don't want to be with me."

She looked down and he raised her chin and unraveled her towel. Walking to the bed, he took a seat while she remained standing. Her skin looked sweet, and he kissed the space between her breasts softly.

Her head fell back and raised slowly again.

In all of the fuck sessions with Lance, she never, ever been kissed there. In fact, she did all she could to make the man think she was scum. Including faking a baby an abortion in the hopes he would leave her alone.

So sex with him was uneventful.

Pulling her a bit closer, he suckled her right breast and then her left. To be so young, Ace had sexed his fair share and knew right about this time her pussy would be wet.

He was right.

Hers was like oil.

Odorless.

Drenched.

Soft.

He pulled her again, and she placed a thigh on the left and right of him, until her pussy covered his dick like a cap on a bottle of water. Her legs rested on the bed, while his feet were planted on the floor as he pumped slowly while looking into her eyes.

"Are you real?" She asked.

He pumped deep.

"Yeah, you're real."

Deeper.

She lowered her head and suckled his bottom lip. Their kiss was so erotic if they weren't more careful, they would cum in an instant and be forced to start all over again.

Something both of them were more than willing to do.

In and out, in and out he pushed until his dick was covered in her juices. He wanted her to remember, forever, this moment with him.

Grabbing her ass cheeks, he squeezed and tapped the walls to the left.

"Hmmm..."

He moved up and then tapped the walls to the right.

"Ahhh..." she said, biting her lip.

Wanting to feel each inch of her body, he whirled as his dick grew stiffer. She felt as good as she looked and that was a plus. His body tingled and hers trembled as they both were about to land.

For Ace it wouldn't be perfect until, "Say my name," he demanded as he pumped in and out a bit faster.

"Hmmm...it feels so..."

"Say my name," he squeezed harder and went deeper.

She looked down at him square on, before wiping the curls from his eyes.

He figured if he heard her say Ace just once, when she felt the way she felt now, that she would forever be his.

Instead, with warm hands on the sides of his face she said, "God."

He smiled.

What could be better than that?

CHAPTER TWENTY
ACE
"They're here."

Ace was on cloud nine.

Not only was the time he spent with Arbella cold, he was certain he was never returning. No matter what Banks said. She would be the nail in the door that would forever close Wales Island for him.

When he opened the motel room he was shocked to see Walid sitting on the edge of the bed.

The room may have been low quality, but Ace did some things to lighten up the feel of the place. In anticipation of Arbella the night before, he cleaned it up and put in fresh towels and washcloths in the bathroom. He also replaced the sheets that came with the room with new linen from a department store. Remembering his maids back home, he even placed carpet freshener down and sprayed so much expensive cologne in the air it smelled aromatic.

None of that mattered at the moment because Walid was livid.

Ace closed the door and smiled. "How did you know I would be here?"

"In the Uber." He readjusted on the bed. "I saw you focusing on the sign. And I knew you needed a place to take your bitch and you ain't got no ID so..."

"I know you mad but–"

"They're here, man. It's time to go."

He frowned. "Who's here?"

"Spacey, Minnesota, Zercy and Blakeslee."

Hearing Blakeslee's name knocked the grin off his face. It was one thing for his brother and sister who were older to come to the states, but he was certain that Banks would destroy the world to bring them all back now.

"Fuck is she here for? Is she safe?"

"Why you care?" Walid shrugged. "You wanted what you wanted. Fuck the rest of us right?"

Silence.

"Why would you drug River, Ace?"

He walked deeper into the room. "She gonna be alright."

"That's not what I asked."

"I needed the car. It's simple."

"Once again it's about you." He paused. "I saw the girl you like a little, Ace. Somebody wants her. And if you aren't careful, a war could be started." He paused. "Who's she dating? What's her background? Do you even know?"

"She won't tell me."

"She won't even tell you her father's name? Or her mother's?"

"Nah, man." Ace said seriously. "She made it clear."

Walid shook his head. "This is wild as fuck."

"Walid, why you mad? You act like I did something to you."

"You get me to come, and I get on board with your plan. And now you out here being disrespectful with your moves. Drugging people and shit. Not telling me where you are." He paused. "I mean if you didn't want my help why you didn't just say it?"

"Okay, I don't want your help. Besides, when I was faking like you, she wasn't interested. Turns out she wants a flashy nigga like me."

Walid grinded his teeth. "It's too late, my nigga."

Ace walked past him and sat on one of the two double beds. "It's her, man. She's the one. And I'm really feeling her."

"I don't give a fuck about that bitch. Our little sister is here. Do you know what father is going to do? All because you couldn't handle being in a place that most people would kill to be in."

"I'm grown, Walid!"

"Ain't nobody trying to hear that shit!"

"And still it's true! I'm eighteen. That means I can do what I want!"

"No, you can't! You're a Wales! That makes you under contract! Period!"

"You sound brainwashed. Was it that shit Joey said?" He laughed. "About father being a gangsta?" He chuckled harder. "I mean think about it, can you really see our father as a kingpin?"

"Yes. I can."

Ace looked at him a bit longer. "Yeah, whatever."

"Say what you want, Ace. You going back."

"No, I'm not!"

Ace realized that arguing with Walid changed his mood for the worst. Literally as he went off, it dawned on him that he was looking at his own face. It was like the good part of him was arguing with the bad part of him to do what was right.

And he wasn't in the mood for any of it.

Suddenly he wished they weren't identical twins anymore.

Ace rose and sat next to him. "I'm not trying to argue with you, brother. But I need you to hear me. I'm not going back to Wales Island."

Upon hearing those words Walid rushed to the nearest wall, and using his fist punched a hole straight through it. Powdered plaster and chips of paint covered his hand and the floor beneath him. "You lied to me!"

Ace wasn't surprised at his reaction.

What most people didn't know was that Walid had a dark side too, that he kept at bay. At least twenty walls were destroyed and repaired on the island that neither Banks nor Mason knew about.

"I didn't lie to you. Shit just different."

"Nah! You lied!" Walid roared. "And you know that's the one thing I can't handle from you."

Ace looked down. "So, what you want me to do? Deny my heart?"

"Your heart? You're Ace Wales! You don't give a fuck about nothing!"

"That's not true!"

"I want you to remember what you had with her last night. I want you to take that feeling and bring it back to the island. And meet somebody who can give you the same thing."

As Ace looked at him he could see tears streaming down his brother's face.

"Please, brother. Come back home with me. I'm begging you."

"When Aliyah and I were first together I knew she would be the one for me." Ace said, looking down and back at him. "But I saw how it was when the three of us were together. I saw that you wanted her and that she appeared to want you too. And I wanted you so happy that I put your feelings over mine."

"What you saying?"

"Aliyah was mine. And I let you have her. Now this girl is for me, Walid. And it ain't got nothing to do with you."

Aliyah was a touchy subject.

Originally it was Ace who was dating her. But it wasn't a long-term relationship. They all met at a party. And it just so happened that Ace spoke to her first, as he usually did with women. And they went out a few times. But no one within five miles of them would be confused that it was Aliyah and Walid that were meant to be.

"Just like I gave you what you wanted, you're going to have to do the same for me now." Ace said softly. "If not, step the fuck up out of my face."

With that he stormed out the door.

CHAPTER TWENTY-ONE
ACE
"I will get back to you."

Arbella was placing her products on her shelves when Ace walked inside. Instead of frowning like she had in the past, now she was grinning ear to ear. She could no longer front.

She was feeling him hard.

"You know you shouldn't be in here right?" She told him, glancing at the door and then back at him. "He could be looking at us."

"Nah, I don't know that."

"I'm serious. Lance will go off if he sees you here."

He readjusted. "You mentioned him before and it's making me think he knows more about me than I know about him. So, who is he? Where is he?"

"I can't tell you that, Ace. I just...I don't know, I just want you to stay safe."

"Fuck it, I'm not afraid of him."

"But you should be though."

On his young rich nigga shit per usual, fear missed him.

The fact that someone wanted her as much as he did, in his mind made pursuing her an adventure. All of his life he was used to getting what he wanted. And who he wanted. And he wasn't going to allow some person he never met change that.

Besides, he recently made a *definite* decision to stay in Baltimore. And he was staying in the city, defying Banks and Mason, for her. That alone was enough reason for him to push buttons.

Even the buttons of a man who he was certain she was no longer feeling.

He grabbed and pulled her closer. "Let me worry about him." He kissed her on the lips, released her and then helped her place products on the shelves.

As he busied himself with work she thought she would do alone, she looked at him. A man this perfect could not be single. "I guess I'm late in asking you this, but do you have a girlfriend?"

"Why? You trying to holla or something?"

She giggled. "I think we're beyond that now." She laughed harder and he liked when he could make that happen. "I'm serious, Ace."

"I never had a girlfriend in my life."

"Wait, you serious?"

"Yep. Never was interested." He thought about Aliyah and allowed the thought to leave his mind.

She placed the gel on the counter and turned to face him. Crossing her arms over her chest she said, "So, you expect me to believe that as long as you lived you never dated someone."

"First of all, I'm only eighteen."

"I had a cousin who had seven girlfriends by the age of eighteen."

He smiled. "Okay I'm going to be real. Where I'm from I can get who I want when I want. But there was nothing or no one I wanted to be my girl until now."

Chills.

"Where are you from, Ace?"

"I can't tell you."

"Why?"

"Because I'm staying here."

She nodded and looked at the chain. "You aren't broke though, are you?"

He grinned and looked down at the pendent. "I just wanna make my own way. With time and hard work, maybe even invest in your future."

She sighed. "Why me though?"

"You sound like you're selling yourself short."

She walked away and sat on one of four chairs towards the back of the shop. It was a place where the construction workers would gather and eat their lunches between building shelves and painting.

He followed and sat next to her.

"I'm not typically the type of girl that boys like you like."

"First off I'm a man."

"I'm serious."

"And so am I." He nodded. "So, help me explain what you mean because I don't get it."

"Look at me, Ace."

"Arbella, I haven't stopped looking at you since I met you. And I'm still waiting on you to answer my question, because I'm confused."

"I always felt that there were girls out there that were prettier than me. Have better bodies than me. And since you look like you walked out of a magazine, I figured you would be more interested in women like that."

He dragged a hand down his face and touched her leg. He was sick of the pretty boy comments.

"I want to say something to you, but I don't need you to respond. As a matter of fact, after I say this, I'm done talking about this shit. Because to disrespect yourself when I'm clearly interested means you saying at the end of the day that I don't have taste. And if I don't have nothing else, taste is it."

She looked down.

"Look at me."

She raised her head.

"If I never met you, if I never saw your face, there would be nothing here to keep me. Because I think you're the finest woman I have ever seen in my life. And I mean that shit. I don't want no dizzy bitch. I want you."

She nodded. "Why do I believe you?"

"The truth has a way of reaching the right spot." He placed a soft finger in her chest.

"So, now you're trying to be all philosophical and shit?"

"It's not that. It's just that there are certain things I don't play with."

"So, now what? I mean we had sex. You are clearly interested in what you see. What do you want with me now?"

"I'm going to be honest, there are some things I'm going to have to deal with over the next couple of days."

His mind wandered to his family that he was certain was descending on Baltimore as he spoke. He knew they would never allow him to stay and that if he wanted to build a life in the city, he would have to fight for the right.

"So, does that mean there is a possibility that we won't get to know each other more?" She said sadly.

"Nah. There's no possibility in my mind that would end with me not getting to know you. And I mean that shit." He stood up and she rose too.

He pulled her toward him, his arms nestling around the small of her back, their bodies became one. And then he kissed her gently. They kissed during sex, but this kiss felt different.

More meaningful.

"I got to make some stops." He continued. "But if we don't see each other over the next few days, just know my family got me hemmed up. But I will get back to you."

"You promise?"

"Let me say this. I'm accustomed to telling people things they want to hear. But I will never ever lie to you. Ever."

She believed him again.

After disconnecting from her body, he exited the store.

With her on his arm he felt he could finally have the life he wanted. Yeah he was spoiled, and yeah he wanted things the way he wanted them. But she had him desiring to settle down.

He was one step away from the Tesla he hijacked the day before when unfortunately for him he never made it. Because he was snatched off the block and thrown in the backseat of a gray pickup truck.

CHAPTER TWENTY-TWO
WALID
"Gas up the jet and let's go."

The Wales clan was frantic.

Not only because Ace had clearly made it known that they could all but suck his dick if they thought he was going back to the island, but also, because they knew Banks and Mason were nearing.

They could feel it in their souls.

Standing in the living room, with the sun shining through the open window, Walid looked at Joey, Spacey, Blakeslee, Minnesota and Zercy.

"I know what you're saying but I don't think we should move like that," Spacey said, yelling at Joey.

"Nigga, you been living in paradise and now you want to try to tell me how to move?" Joey responded. "We not on the island. These are the streets."

"Why do you keep saying that dumb shit?" Minnesota asked Joey. "You sound jealous."

"Exactly!" Spacey said. "Especially since you chose to stay behind."

"Wait, why does everybody hate where we live?" Blakeslee added.

"It's not that," Zercy said touching her leg softly. "They always fight when they get together like–."

"Stop!" Walid yelled at everyone. "Just, just shut the fuck up!"

Everybody looked up at Walid, believing he went mad. He had been standing there for over a minute but not one of them seemed to notice.

"If Ace wants to stay here, let him."

"Wait, what?" Joey responded. "Because I thought you were the one who wanted him to come back most of all."

Walid looked down. "I love my brother. But I'm tired of chasing him around. He made a promise to me. He broke that promise. And now all I want to do is get back to my wife and kid."

"You guys aren't married." Blakeslee said.

"Leave it alone." Minnesota responded.

"I'm serious! He told me if I helped him get the girl he would come back to Wales Island. But he fucked her and acting brand new. So, he lied. And that makes me look at him differently."

"Listen, little brother. I know you mad with Ace. But there's no possibility in the realm of possibilities that would include us leaving him here. You don't understand the drama that's about to occur right now." Spacey looked at Joey and Minnesota. "But we do."

They nodded.

It took everything in Minnesota's power not to shit herself.

"I don't care about that. Gas up the jet and let's go."

"And I just said I can't do that. We got to find him. If we know where he is and then can tell pops that, to be honest that would be enough for me. But going back empty handed ain't happening."

Walid was furious.

As a matter of fact, not being able to get back to Wales Island had him realizing how helpless he was in Baltimore. The idea or the thought of not seeing Aliyah again was too much to bear.

He would learn how to fly for sure.

"So, what do we have to do to get up in the air?" Walid asked. "Because I'm sick of wasting time."

"It's simple. We have to find Ace." Joey said.

"And we have to find him now." Spacey continued.

"What happens if we don't? Because I saw how he looked. His obsession with this chick is massive."

"Let's just say there's a side of pops that you haven't seen," Spacey warned. "A side that you don't want to see to be honest. When he gets mad he gets vicious. And anybody can get caught up in his wrath. Even his own kids."

CHAPTER TWENTY-THREE

BANKS

"The whole city would burn down."

Banks chartered his luxury jet through the skies as if he actually had wings. The luscious white clouds were nonfactors for the power of the aircraft, which meant the ride was smooth.

As Mason sat next to him, Banks thought about many things.

For instance, what he would do if something happened to his offspring. Although he knew he could be a bit much when it came to keeping them protected, in his mind it was for their own good.

After all, because they came from money, in his opinion, they didn't know how vulnerable that made them to predators. He realized that he was probably using the law of attraction wrong, but their safety was always a primary concern.

Could he be willing unwanted shit into his existence?

Now that he thought about it briefly, perhaps worrying so much was the reason he found himself going back to a country he never thought he'd return to.

"I think I'm going to ask Luciana to marry me when we get back." Mason said, looking ahead at the sky.

Banks nodded.

"It's been a long time since I felt like being with a woman exclusively. And I think she's the one. I really do."

"I'm happy for you." Banks didn't look his way.

"Are you?"

"I get it." Banks continued. "She takes care of you. Thinks your jokes are funny. What more could you want in a woman?"

"What about you? Will you ever settle down again? I mean let's be real you don't have many years left in you. And I haven't seen you with a woman since we got to the island. Don't you want the dream you planned for us? Don't you want happily ever after too?" He chuckled.

"I don't think I'll ever fall in love again."

"When were you ever in love?" Mason pressed.

Banks looked at him and looked away.

Mason looked away too.

"I'm focused on the family." Banks continued.

"Well, you shouldn't close yourself off that way."

"Like I said, the only thing I'm thinking about is giving my children the life I never had in Baltimore.

It consumes all of my thoughts. Everyday. Every minute. Every second."

"What if this isn't what they see for themselves?"

He frowned and looked at him.

"I'm serious, Banks. They're older now. Grown adults. You can't give them what they aren't willing to accept."

"I started back taking hormone therapy."

"I knew." Mason said, looking downward and then out ahead of him at the skies.

"If what the doctor said is true, that I could do further damage to my brain, then it's a possibility that I may die. And if that happens, I want to make sure that my children are happy."

"Have you ever thought about how losing you would make me feel?"

Silence.

"You're my oldest friend."

"True." Banks nodded. "So, you of all people should know how much being fully me, means to me."

Mason sighed, "You know what, I'm not even humoring this. You aren't going anywhere."

"That may or may not be true. But I need them to know that what they think they want will destroy their lives."

"How can you be so sure?"

"You act like you aren't from the city," Banks said, tapping a few buttons on his control panel. "Everything vile, hateful and fucked up happened to us in the states, Mason."

He nodded.

"We lost our sons. Wives and–."

"Some of that was by our own hands." Mason reminded him.

"True. But now we don't have to deal with it anymore. We can live the lives we always dreamed of but not in America."

"That's not everybody's dream, Banks. That's what I'm trying to get you to understand. I think if you finally got it, things would be easier for you."

"I'll never understand. I'm telling you straight up."

"One day they will hate you beyond return for trying to control every aspect of their lives, Banks. Is that what you want?"

"As long as they're safe, it's something I'm willing to face."

"What we went through was rough." Mason said. "It's true..."

"Worse than rough." Banks corrected.

"But that was our reality. It doesn't mean that it has to be theirs too. Maybe they can find a better way of living in–"

"Can you look me in the eyes and say seriously that you think Ace is ready to live in Baltimore on his own?" Banks interrupted.

Silence.

"I'm asking honestly?" Banks continued.

Mason sat back in his seat and dragged two hands down his face. "Nah, that nigga would wreak havoc and the whole city would burn down."

"Exactly. So..." Banks' eyes widened as he saw a warning flash on his panel.

"What's wrong?"

"Something is going on with the engine."

"What does that mean?"

Banks looked at him and back at the skies. "I think the plane is going down."

CHAPTER TWENTY-FOUR WALID

"Do you resent her for it?"

The brothers, including the brother-in-law, stood on the patio. The sisters and sister-in-law worked in the kitchen to prepare meals no one had a stomach to eat.

Shit was finna get serious!

And everyone was concerned.

"So, what we do is talk to her and tell her that although she may be feeling Ace it's in her best interest to step the fuck off." Joey suggested, slapping the back of his hand into the other. "She may get a little upset but at the end of the day, if we apply pressure, she may get the picture."

"I don't think it will work." Spacey said, shaking his head from left to right.

"I disagree," Joey added.

"Especially if we make it known that this is not up for discussion." Zercy added.

"I don't think we should go that route either." Walid said.

Everyone looked at him.

"Why not?" Joey asked.

"I think we should wait and let him come to her at the shop. We talk sense into him, not her because getting her in the mix is wrong."

"Maybe you been on that island too long but–"

"There this jealous ass nigga go with the island talk again," Spacey interjected.

"Being on the island has given me a clear mind you would or could never understand living here." Walid replied.

Spacey nodded in agreement.

"And I'm telling you, confronting her the way y'all talking about won't work." Walid continued.

"Why are you so adamant about it?"

"First off if y'all want Ace to come back with us, then disrespecting somebody he's feeling is going to do nothing but push him away."

Suddenly he was making the best sense out of all the brothers.

"Let's watch her shop. And see what happens. If Ace shows up, we make our presence known. If he doesn't want to come with us, we follow where he's resting his head because he's not at the motel anymore. I checked. And then give the information to father. After that we go home."

Zercy and Spacey sat in the car on the west end of the shop. In the car alone, they were forced to speak.

"Listen, I know you don't like me," Zercy said making sure to keep his eyes on the beauty store. "But we should cut all this shit out."

"Never said I didn't like you."

"Then what is it?" He looked over at him.

"You come with a lot of baggage." Spacey melted into the seat.

Zercy laughed once.

Spacey looked at him and then back at the shop. "What part was funny?"

"Everything the Wales family does is baggage. I mean look at what's happening now."

Spacey readjusted his dick a little. "Look, Minnesota when she was younger started a lot of shit. Got folks hemmed up in ways you can't imagine."

"I'm hip." Zercy nodded.

"Hip, huh?"

"Seriously. Me and Minnie talk about the past all the time. I know some of the tales."

"Be careful calling her Minnie. She doesn't like it."

"She seems to be quite alright when I say it."

Spacey felt angrier than he had in a long time. "Look, we here to watch the shop. So, do me a favor and don't say shit else to me."

"Done."

Night dropped on the block as Walid and Joey sat in a car on the east end of the shop. Across from Zercy and Spacey. Although both cars waited for five hours outside the shop, neither had yet to show up.

"You know I didn't mean no disrespect 'bout the island thing right, Walid?"

"Yes you did. That's why you keep saying it." He paused. "So, why didn't you leave?"

"She didn't want to." He sighed.

"Your wife?"

"Who else?"

Walid nodded "Do you resent her for it?"

Joey cleared his throat and decided to skip the subject. "So...how is he?"

"Who?"

"Pops. And I'm not talking about Mason because I know that's what y'all little niggas call him."

"You talk to him all the time."

"And he doesn't seem happy. Which is why I'm asking."

Walid sighed. "We throw these parties once a month. I'm talking about people from all over come to eat our food, dance to the music and spend time with our family. There are businesses that have been created for these parties...that's how popular they are. It's known on nearby islands as Wales Night."

Joey smiled imagining the beauty.

"But with all of the celebrations, father never seems happy. A few times I caught him staring at pops and his new girl, and I wonder if he's looking at the love they got brewing because he wants it for himself."

Joey knew the complicated story surrounding his father and Mason, but he would never say a word. "Wow...I hoped he would finally be at peace."

"How did we come to be, Joey? Me and Ace. I mean, what's the story between my father and pops? Like, I know we share both of their blood but I'm not a hundred percent sure how. When I try to wrap my mind around the possibilities, it doesn't make sense."

"Listen, that's a conversation I'm not prepared to have at–."

"Never mind." He waved the air.

"Listen, man."

Walid sighed.

"I'm not willing to go there now, Walid. But I promise you, before you leave Baltimore you will know the truth."

Walid nodded and then looked out ahead.

Another hour had passed and still Aliyah didn't show her pretty face.

"Something ain't right," Joey said.

"I agree."

"It's been a long time since I felt fear but right now, in this fucking car, I'm legit scared to death."

"Me too."

CHAPTER TWENTY-FIVE
BANKS
"And then I'll be back in the air."

After a dangerous, rough landing, Banks and Mason were accepted into a small airport in Mexico. At first air traffic control wouldn't grant him entry but when he said the name Nicolas Rivera, the small town opened up to him.

The moment the plane landed, eight pickup trucks in various states of old and damn near broken, pulled out. Within seconds of parking, they exited the vehicle and surrounded the luxury aircraft.

From the cockpit, the moment Mason saw them on the runway he said, "I told you we shouldn't have called him."

"It was an engine failure. We had no choice."

Reluctantly Banks and Mason exited the aircraft. Standing in the middle of the armed man was Nicolas Rivera. He was seventy something years old and had a pep in his step of a teenager.

Walking up to Banks in a rich Mexican accent he said, "The great Banks Wales. It's so amazing to have you in my country again." He raised his arms and spun, basically doing the most.

He stank horribly.

Banks shook his hand. "You know I couldn't stay away for too long." Actually, he would have preferred not to ever leave his island, but he was playing the part.

Nicolas pointed a soiled nail at him, "But you did though. You did stay away."

Mason and Banks looked at him and could smell the funk and liquor stemming from his breath.

Banks shifted a little. "I want to introduce you to my oldest friend–"

"Mason!" Nicolas said, cutting him off. "We all know the great Mr. Mason Louisville. There have been bottles emptied while listening to your tales in Baltimore."

Mason stepped forward with the use of his cane and shook his hand firmly. He wanted it to be known that although he walked with assistance he could still eat, fight and fuck.

"Thank you for inviting us into the airport." Banks said. "I'll pay any of your men to help me repair my aircraft ten times what they would normally charge. And then I'll be back in the air."

Two ashy palms faced Banks. "Not so fast. We want you as guests into our home first."

"Nicolas, as much as I would like to stay, I'm going to have to be honest. My sons may be in trouble in America. And I have to see to it that–"

"Aren't your children grown men and women?"

"Not all of them. And that's not the point." Mason said.

"Maybe. But right now, my point appears to be this, you need help. And I'm in a position to help you. All I'm asking for is a little grace. If you can do that, I'll repair your aircraft and you can be on the way. If not..."

Many guns cocked in the air.

"Then I'm not sure what will happen."

Banks shook his head.

Mason walked away.

CHAPTER TWENTY-SIX
WALID

"You're waiting on ammunition."

Walid, River, Minnesota, Blakeslee, Spacey, Joey and his guard, stood on the patio discussing the defeat of not finding Ace.

Zercy was not present.

Most drank bottle after bottle, while trying to devise a plan to bring Ace home, but Walid wasn't in the mood to be drunk.

At first he wanted to go home, but after not being able to find Arbella, he was now concerned that something else was happening with his brother.

And he wanted answers.

"I'm going back to her shop." Walid announced.

"Maybe.... maybe we can wait 'till...'till the morning." Joey slurred. "To give us a chance to sober up."

"You can wait till the morning if you want to but I'm going back to the shop." He looked at everyone. "So, the only question is whose car can I use?"

River rose. "I'm going with you."

Minnesota sat in one of Joey's many guest rooms with tears running down her face. After the first stakeout at Arbella's shop, everyone returned to Joey's crib with the exception of her husband.

Not only was it embarrassing but it was also mad disrespectful.

Three hours later, after being deep in worry, he finally entered the room. Drunk and smelling of a different kind.

She repositioned herself on the bed and looked at him as he stood near the open doorway. "For what I'm about to say to you, you may want to shut that shit." She wiped her tears away roughly. "I don't want one of my brother's fucking you up."

"Aren't they my brothers too?"

"Ask them and see."

He shook his head. "I've never known one of your brothers to be violent."

"Yeah, aight." He closed the door and she laughed. "Where were you?"

"I'm sorry I'm just getting in. I decided to get up with some old friends I haven't seen in a while and one thing led to another."

"Led to another what."

"Minnesota, I don't want to do this with you." He paused. "Not tonight."

"If not now than when?"

Her words were heavy and laced with insinuation. As far as she was concerned he had gotten tired of paradise a long time ago. And Ace making his escape was all the excuse he needed to come back too.

What troubled her was not that he was out having a good time. But if her feelings were right, he wasn't interested in returning. She never met so many people who wanted to escape from Heaven on Earth in her life.

"I'm waiting on an answer, Zercy."

"No, you're waiting on ammunition."

"I have no idea what you're talking about."

"Your mind is already made up. You're sure I did the things that you're thinking about. Now you just want an excuse to fight. The thing is I don't feel like fighting." He removed his shoes followed by his socks and then his pants. Next he pulled back the covers on his side of the bed and got in, as if he were clean.

"If you don't want to be with me anymore just say the words, Zercy."

"I'm not going to say what I'm not feeling."

"Then what is it? Fucking talk to me!"

"I lived with you on that island for over twelve years. Maybe we should stay here for a little while and get reconnected with what we knew before everything changed. If I want that, could it be wrong?"

"You know I can't do that."

"Actually, I don't."

When my father comes, and it will be soon, the last thing he will do is allow us to stay in this place. Every hour that we spend here puts our lives in danger. And I thought you understood that already."

"Everybody who had beef with y'all niggas are probably long gone."

"Oh, I know you drunk now, because you talking crazy."

"Minnesota..."

"Probably, is not enough for safety, Zercy. We gotta get out of America!"

Silence.

Taking a deep breath she said, "Are you saying that you aren't coming back with me? Tell me now. I have a right to know."

"What I'm telling you is that I'm done talking about it." He rolled over and turned off the light.

In her mind she had gotten her answer.

BLAKESLEE

Since everybody was drunk, Blakeslee sat in the front of the house with Joey's young guard, Push, who was overlooking the property. His purpose was to make sure no one drove up without his knowing and Blakeslee, thinking he was attractive, decided to keep him company.

"I'm mentally older than most people I know." She said sitting on a step picking at a small scar on her knee.

"I don't doubt it."

"Ace told me all the time. It was one of the reasons why he likes talking to me the most. He said I had a good ear. And can listen and understand so many things he says."

"That's good to know. Most young girls your age only think about boys, clothes and social media."

She looked down and sighed. "We aren't allowed to go on social media. Not the younger ones anyway."

"Wait, so you're not online?"

She shook her head from left to right. "Father doesn't allow us to do anything connected to the outside. But Walid had a phone. And sometimes I would go online and look at the world anyway. He didn't know it though. When I couldn't use his phone I would use Aliyah's instead."

"Wow. I guess you're willing to do whatever you can to stay connected."

She sighed and dragged her long hair out of her face. It cascaded down her back like curtains. "I have to teach myself stuff."

"Like what?"

"Well, I tried to talk to Ace about it but he got mad. It was the first time I seen him mad too. So mad he said he would slap me in the face if I asked him that again. I only said it though because I saw it on social media."

"What was it?"

"I asked him how to suck dick."

He frowned. "I don't know what you mean."

"Yes you do." She grinned. "I can see it on your face." She pointed at him and laughed harder.

Suddenly the front door opened, and Joey grabbed her by the wrist and pulled her inside. He told her repeatedly to stay in the house but she didn't listen. Keeping up with her was like trying to control five puppies.

"Fuck are you doing outside?"

"Just talking." She shrugged.

"But I told you, you need to stay in the house. What part of that didn't you get?"

"You may be my brother but I don't know you. And I won't tolerate you talking to me that way."

For some reason Joey suddenly understood why Banks maintained the control over the family he did. He could say with 100% clarity that if he left his eyes off of her she would be trouble.

"You may not know me. But I'm still your older brother." He pointed in her chest. "And I'm willing to do whatever I gotta do to make sure you're safe. Some of those things you won't like. But if you don't want to call me on it, I suggest you stay in this house. This is the final warning."

"You know, Walid said you gave Ace a warning too."

Joey was flushed with embarrassment.

"He didn't listen. So, what makes you think I will?"

"What you just–."

"If you want to be more like father, try being a little firmer. Maybe then I'll believe you." She bounced down the hallway and out of sight.

WALID

The sun had risen as Walid and River maintained their gaze on the shop. Walid was hoping that at some point Ace would make an appearance.

Nothing.

Already he missed his brother and hated the final words they said to one another at the motel. It was all so dumb. Suddenly he wished he hadn't wasted such time on frivolous arguing.

When River's phone rang, she seemed visibly upset. "I have to take this."

He nodded and continued to focus on the shop. But it didn't mean he wasn't listening. All night she received calls and text messages. Each appearing to make her more uncomfortable than the next.

"What's up?" She said into the phone.

Silence.

"Tomorrow huh?"

Silence.

"I'll be there." She hung up and dragged a hand down her face.

Walid didn't have any room for anybody else's struggles. But at the same time, he was bored and could use a distraction from the thoughts in his mind. "What's going on?"

"Nothing."

Walid nodded, catching the hint.

"Actually, a friend of mine, Tinsley, is coming home."

Walid scratched his scalp. "Tinsley. I know the name."

She looked over at him, her back against the window. "You do?"

"Yes. Father set him up with an apartment, a car and a banking account. For when he comes home. He's in prison or something right?"

Her jaw dropped.

"He said he was a good friend too."

Her eyes widened and rage overcame her. "Are you sure about that?"

"Ace and father spent hours going over business ventures, banking accounts and shit like that. And I remember Ace talking to me about the name Tinsley. Said he had given him enough money never to have to work again for two lifetimes. Which was odd because we were the only people who had more money than him at the time. But Ace said father looked at him like a nephew. So that made it different."

River shook her head, and a look of deviousness took over. "Thanks for the info."

"No doubt."

CHAPTER TWENTY-SEVEN
ARBELLA
"What are you willing to pay?"

Victoria Valentine sat near a large open window, overlooking her serene garden. Despite being horribly disfigured, for her, it was a small price to pay to escape Tyrone, Arbella's father.

And now, as her daughter sat across from her with alternating stares between her mother and the garden, she waited for her mother's wisdom. Victoria was often called a coot or crazy, but they didn't know that she placed all of her energy into greater things.

Into places that the world could not touch.

When Arbella's phone rang for the fiftieth time, with Lance's number, she sighed. She refused to answer any of his calls, wanting him to leave her alone so she could be with Ace.

And yet it appeared easier said than done.

"I had an apartment in New York before you were born."

"I didn't know you lived there." She dropped her cell into her purse.

"I did." She paused. "And the person who owned the building said I could stay for as long as I wanted.

Originally I asked Dave, the owner, if I could stay for a couple of days. But I liked the place so much that days became weeks and before long a month passed." She shook her head. "Only one month."

Arbella resituated knowing her mother was about to drop wisdom on her that she could apply to her own life.

"One night, on the 30th day, I just got off from work. It was dark and I was in my bed preparing to sleep when the front door opened. And then my room door. The owner, a large man standing about 6'3 and weighing 450 pounds walked in. I was scared. And yet that word doesn't hold the weight of how I felt inside."

"What did he want?"

"He said, *'have you decided what you are willing to pay?'"*

Arbella leaned forward totally engrossed into the story.

"I asked, *'what are you doing in my room?' 'Your room?'* He spoke. *'You haven't paid a dollar since you've lived here for the past month.'* He said. *'That's because you said I could stay here and at the end of the month make a decision on what to pay you.'"*

Arbella was fearful of what happened to her mother in the past.

"*'I didn't lie. I will pay'*, I told him. '*What are you willing to pay now?*'"

Arbella continued to focus on her mother's disfigured face. She had been burned so badly, her nose was barely in place and her left eye was shut.

Still, she was the calmest person Arbella knew.

"I was so excited about living in New York that I hadn't given much consideration to what I would give him to stay in his apartment. And since he didn't bother me, it slipped my mind until that moment."

"What happened next?"

"I paid the price of living there with the most violent sex I had ever experienced in my life. He bit me on the face. My back. My thighs. I begged for him to just have sex with me but that didn't come until eighteen hours later. Instead of penetrating me sexually he used brooms and stick handles to enact the worst things known to man on my body. To be honest I didn't think I would ever have any children. And yet here you are."

A tear rolled down Arbella's cheek.

"You're in a relationship with one of the meanest young men in Baltimore. You stayed in this relationship because you liked how it made you feel. You were the envy of your friends. Even family members looked at your life wanting what they saw for themselves. They lusted after Lance and his strikingly good looks. But you knew that being with him meant living in a mental building that you didn't want to be. And now to leave him means you'll have to pay."

Arbella was shaken.

"My daughter, determine what you're willing to pay. And pay no more than that. Leave him and never return. Not for any reason. Even that of your father's."

CHAPTER TWENTY-EIGHT
BANKS
"What do you want with us?"

It was supposed to be a party.

But the land where the event was held was damp and soft. Every step brought with it a cloud of mosquitoes and various insects that seemed to leave everyone alone but Mason and Banks.

While Mason tapped at his face and legs in an effort to escape their bites, Banks was razor focused. Even if they had teeth he would not have flinched.

In this moment he used the time to remember every face. Every object and even people who stood in the background, looking at them as if they were a feast only fit for a king.

Women who smelled of disease and dirt danced around them which made the mood more intense. Their faces may have been slightly wiped but between their legs were spoiled like rotten fruit. And although Banks and Mason both wanted them as far away from them as possible, it annoyed them further.

Mason shoved woman after woman out of his way, as they sat on warped benches connected to a picnic table. While Banks gave them no emotion. Eventually they just left him alone and focused on

Mason instead. Because even in his rage he was at least responding.

After a few hours, finally Nicolas sat in front of him. On the table was a feast of echt meals that looked spoiled. Barbacoa, concha's, black beans, churros and more. All laced with flies and bugs as if they were pepper.

Banks analyzed everything happening for a moment, and when he got the exact data needed to know what was going on he said, "What do you want from me Nicolas?"

Nicolas frowned, "My friend, this is a–."

"I've expressed to you I'm not here for games. My family is in danger, and I must leave. Either you help me or let me go. We will find our way."

"When you were last in Mexico, before your father was killed, it was I who gave him his fourth pack. He had problems getting work from his other distributor, so he contacted me for help. And I made a way to get it to him through Texas and beyond. You could say I was responsible for your rise. Now my resources are dried up. And no one will deal with me. In a sense, I need you."

"Why will no one deal with you?"

"Does it matter?"

"To me it does."

"Let's just say I made a few moves that people took the wrong way. People are all so sensitive now." He slapped at the air. "The thing is I still have a family and I have people to take care of. And I'm not going to be able to do that unless my reach is a little longer."

"Nigga, what do you want?" Mason responded, unable to hold back any longer. "You talking a lot but haven't said shit."

"I want to tap into the market in America."

"I'm out the game." Banks admitted.

"Yeah, ain't you heard? My nigga sells curls now."

Nicolas nodded. "Yeah, I heard that. But the heart wants what it wants."

"And my heart wants to reconnect with my children to make sure they're okay."

"Again, with the children, buddy." He chuckled. "They're grown."

"And so are you," Mason said. "But you begging for help nonetheless."

Nicolas rolled his eyes and focused back on Banks. "If you taught them well enough I'm sure they can take care of themselves. But this is about money."

"He's a billionaire. He's good."

"Your friend has lips," Nicolas warned.

"Nigga, what?"

Banks placed a hand on Mason's arm, calming him down.

"If I tell you no, which I am fully prepared to do, what is your next move?" Banks responded.

"I guess there will be nothing I could do right?" He threw his hands up.

"Well let me think about it." Banks said.

"You have twenty-four hours."

The fact that there was a time frame on the request that extended longer than what he was willing to spend in the country, irritated Banks even more. Every hour that passed with his bloodline being in a state that he felt wanted them dead, drove him insane.

Banks was always aware that he was a control freak. But it's because he wholeheartedly believed that there were people out there that meant to destroy him and those he loved.

And Nicolas proved his point.

When Nicolas got up from the table, as if nothing was wrong and entertained two women who smelled of fish, another stranger walked up to the table and sat next to him.

Banks did what he always did and assessed the stranger as much as possible. Refusing to speak first, he waited for him to state his business.

"If you don't tell Nicolas yes tonight, he will kill you both within the next eight hours. And then he will brag to everyone about how he murdered the great Banks Wales and Mason Louisville. He'll figure that may be enough to make your enemies open the lines necessary for him to get rich in America."

Mason was pissed.

Banks was not surprised.

"So, what do you want with us?" Banks asked.

"I suggest you both do a better job of faking like you're enjoying yourselves. And then my men will pour so much liquor down Nicolas' throat that he won't get a chance to give the order that his hitters are waiting on."

"What's the order?" Mason asked.

"To spill and possibly drink your blood."

Suddenly the flies didn't seem so annoying, and Mason was prepared to put on a performance. "After we fake it, what happens next?" Mason questioned.

"I'll sneak you out. And then you'll come with me."

CHAPTER TWENTY-NINE
WALID

"Brother, I wish I could give you more right now."

Walid stood in the shower with the water running over his body, thinking about his girl and son. He wondered if she was worried and if he had unknowingly triggered the autoimmune disease that tormented her for years.

At first he was ready to risk it all, but the trip taught him what truly mattered. Family. The one he was building. Not the one he was born into. And he was certain that he would never make the mistake again, to ruin his world for his twin.

The only good part about the trip came to him in an odd way.

He realized that being in the states allowed him to rebuild connections with his brothers, sisters and even his brother-in-law Zercy. He learned new things about them that living in a mansion with rooms so far apart you might as well live alone, never allowed.

Still, he wanted to return to his family.

His girl and son and he would do that, at all costs.

He was just about to get out of the shower when suddenly a sharp pain hit him in the stomach. It was so great it caused him to double over and required him to seek a place to sit immediately.

Naked and wet, he tumbled out of the shower, and flopped on the closed toilet seat. With the water running he gripped his stomach even more to relieve himself of the pain.

What was he feeling?

And then it dawned on him.

Something was wrong.

Something was very wrong!

He recalled a movie that he watched not even a year ago. It talked about how twins could feel the pain of the other, whether mental or physical. At that time, both of them recalled different occurrences where Walid would stub his toe and Ace would say what are you doing? Due to feeling the same pain.

It caused them to want to go deeper and before long, they found out what the strange phenomena was that connected them. On the surface it made sense. They shared the exact same DNA.

This meant that something was wrong with Ace.

He was in danger.

If he was still alive.

Spacey and Minnesota looked at Walid closely as he expressed what happened in the shower. It wasn't that they didn't believe him. It was just that everyone was preparing for Banks' return only for him to tear each of them a new asshole.

Each sibling in their minds realized that once he discovered they all fled Wales Island, that when he got a hold of them, that they would all return to a prison that he would impose.

So, they were trying to get their shit in order.

And then there were their personal relationships that were in dire straits.

Joey fought with Sydney on a regular basis. Zercy and Minnesota separated bedrooms, although he tried desperately to get back into her good graces and bed, after realizing his error. And Blakeslee was angry that they wouldn't allow her to get on social media to find her new boyfriend. She was also missing her nephews back on the island, and most of all Ace.

Even River, who was not family but connected, was dealing with the fact that Tinsley had lied about how much Banks had been doing for him, and she was starting to look at him a different way. Mainly because he used the fact that he needed her to financially care for him, while he was doing time for her crime.

At the end of the day everybody was occupied and so the story about how a twin was feeling the phantom pain of another wasn't on their list of concerns.

"Brother, I wish I could give you more right now." Spacey said. "I really do. But I have a feeling that someone spotted me when we were out looking for Ace. And now my baby mother who hasn't spoken to Riot in about two years knows I'm back. And that's drama I don't need right now."

Just that moment his brother-in-law, Zercy, walked up behind Minnesota and said, "Can we talk? Please."

She looked at her husband, rolled her eyes and focused back on her brother. "Listen, Ace is for the streets now," she paused. "The sooner you know that shit the better off you'll be."

"Yeah, just let it go." Spacey added. "Because it's out of our hands right now."

Without saying goodbye, the three of them left, and Walid was faced with dealing with his grief alone.

Fuck them!

He would hunt for his brother by himself.

Walid didn't know whose luxury vehicle he was in until he popped open the glove compartment to get a napkin. It was then that he saw a family photo full of vanilla-colored faces.

It was Sydney's car.

And it would do.

No matter what happened or how late it got, he was going to sit on that store until Arbella showed her face. To his surprise he waited less than fifteen minutes and she was there.

He worked himself up in preparation so long to wait hours, that the timeframe threw him off guard a little.

The first thing he noticed was how beautiful she was. When he initially saw her, it was briefly because she remained in the car, and he did too due to being irritated with Ace. He could finally see why his brother was feeling her although in his opinion she wasn't bad enough to leave paradise for.

The moment she parked her car and entered her store he took a deep breath. It was quite possible that she had no idea what happened to Ace and so he had to be cool. Like his father, Banks, who always seemed ready for any situation.

Five minutes later he exited the car and entered the beauty store.

The moment Arbella saw his face, she dropped the box of pens on the floor and ran up to him. Her body trembled as she held him tightly.

At that moment it was clear.

Not only was Ace missing. But it was obvious to Walid that she had no idea where he was. This brought a type of dread to him he wasn't prepared to handle.

For some reason he recalled Ace telling him that she was adamant about not speaking about her ex-boyfriend's whereabouts. Who on all accounts was extremely jealous.

Could he have his brother?

If he was going to get the information that he needed out of her, he had to ditch himself.

He had to become, Ace.

Separating from him she looked up into his beautiful face. And then she slapped him. "Where were you? You said you would never leave me!" She wiped tears away, but they continued to flood. "Why do that to me?"

The slap didn't hurt him at all. "I'm sorry. I had some things that came up and–"

"You don't do people like that! I thought something happened to you! I thought you were...you were..."

This was the conversation he was willing to have. Walking closer and massaging the sides of her arms he looked down at her and said, "You thought I was what?"

She inhaled and exhaled. "Dead."

"Why is that the first thing you thought about?" He glared. "Is it because of your boyfriend?"

"My ex! I'm officially done with him."

Walid had to position his next question carefully. Although the last time he spoke to Ace he told him that she was unwilling to share the history of her people, what if that changed? And he didn't get an update from Ace.

If she mentioned that she already told him, that could put her on pause. Especially if Ace told her he had a twin brother.

"Where does he live? Your ex?" He grew serious and his stare almost turned cold but he didn't give a fuck. "I need you to stop playing around and tell me now."

"I can't do–"

Suddenly a loud explosion pounded on the property.

The sound was deafening and the vibration painful.

Instinctually, he covered her body with his own, as products, plastering and shelving flew everywhere, also weighing down on his back. The smoke alarm went off as the store went mostly dark.

Lifting himself up, debris fell off his physique. He helped her to her feet and pushed away so much of the building and its structure which collapsed on them, that he was surprised they were even alive.

Coughing and helping her out of the disaster, he was relieved to see his brother through the glass door trying to get inside.

Walid helped her out and she cried as the air hit her lungs.

"What the fuck happened?" Joey yelled helping him and her exit the destroyed property.

"We gotta get out of here," Walid coughed, as he ushered her toward Joey's car.

But Joey was pressed for answers and said, "What happen, Wa–."

Walid, roughly tugged on his shoulder, brought his lips to his ear and said, "She thinks I'm Ace."

Not knowing why he lied, Joey continued to help them to the car. He was mostly relieved that his kid brother was alive while also realizing that what he was witnessing was a hit.

But on who?

Once inside the car, Joey rushed away from the scene with Walid in the back and the girl crying in his arms.

Walid didn't know, but after Blakeslee called Joey out for not being like Banks, Joey put trackers in every car on his property, believing that if someone took one, even Blakeslee who was getting hot in the pants, that he would know their whereabouts.

The thing was, Joey didn't tell a soul.

And his instincts paid off.

CHAPTER THIRTY
BANKS
"What happens next has to be strategic."

Jago's home was small but cared for greatly. It sat on a large farm which yielded crops of all types of produce, including fruit and cacao.

He had a beautiful family. A wife, one daughter and three strapping sons. And they all doted over Jago and his present company.

In the wee hours of the morning, they tended to Banks and Mason as they sat in his small kitchen, going over the next move.

"Why exactly can't we go to the plane right now?" Mason questioned as he sipped some of the best coffee he'd ever had in his life. "With Nicolas being drunk it seems to me that now is the time to make the move."

"Nicolas may be under some woman, but Nicolas' men are there. So, what happens next has to be strategic."

Banks considered his statement and said, "I remember Nicolas vaguely. I had limited dealings with him when my father was alive. But I remember him being smarter than this. He knows fucking with me is dangerous. What changed?"

Jago sat back in his seat and took a deep breath. "He became known as *the man with no morals.* Although coke was his first line of business, after being given ten million dollars to take out a family that was in the way of one of the biggest drug lords Mexico had ever seen, he was surprised at how much money he could make in the business of murder."

Banks listened attentively.

"Suddenly he didn't feel like having to weigh or count cocaine bricks. He thought it was easier to murder because once the job was done the money was in hand. And so, he began to take pride in how he hunted and took out what he deemed as prey. He also took pride in being the one that would take any hit. Even kids."

Mason shook his head. "Funky ass nigga."

"One day he went too far though. He murdered an innocent mother who was giving birth to her daughter in a maternity unit. Even the vilest of vile had a problem with that move. And so, no one came to him about any other requests. It was as if the underworld made an agreement, that he was too dirty for them. He was in a sense cursed and to get involved with him meant that your business would dry up too."

Mason smiled. "Sounds like they got it right."

"So, he tried to ease back into the coke world. But he was only able to do a few hand-to-hand jobs. Nothing that would net him the money he had become accustomed to. Had it not been for his habit of sex with whores and expensive tequila, he could have lived a great life off of his money. After all, he earned millions from his trade."

"And that's why he won't let us leave." Mason said.

"He has nothing to lose. And doing business with a man who has nothing to lose is dangerous."

"Out of everyone you know, is there anyone who can work on a plane, despite his men being there?"

"Are you asking if I know anyone who would be ready for a war?"

Silence.

"I know a few people, but they are all afraid of Nicolas. He has proven himself to be a worthy adversary."

"I'm willing to pay whatever. My accountants can wire money anywhere in less than an hour."

"I'm sure you realize it's deeper than that, Banks. What's the good of having money if everything you love is gone? And that's the kind of trouble that he can create. He will murder your family and anyone you've ever looked at."

"So, you brought us here to tell us stories?" Banks responded. "Because I have to say, I have Netflix at home."

"I brought you here to save your life."

"The only way our lives can be saved is if we're in the air. Every moment spent here is putting us in more danger." He pointed stiff fingers into the table. "I need to get my plane fixed. So, if you aren't willing to do it then–"

"You know, I would think you would be a little more grateful." He lowered his brow.

Banks didn't trust him. "Every man has a price. Fuck gratitude and tell me yours."

"Yeah, what do you want?" Mason added.

Jago leaned closer, just as his wife replenished their cups with more strong and delicious coffee.

"I have made some moves in the background that Nicolas doesn't know about. Moves that contradict what he stands for."

"What do you stand for?" Mason asked.

"I want him gone. He has made advances toward my wife and it has made me uncomfortable. Since at one point I considered him a friend."

"Sounds like you have bad taste in associates," Mason said.

"Maybe. Anyway, for a while I was able to do these things and stay under the radar. But someone in his camp, a confidant, recently made it known to me that he doesn't trust me either."

"Does anyone trust anyone?" Mason responded.

"Nicolas not trusting you could mean a sneak attack in any number of places. And so, I need my family to be somewhere safe. In a place that his influence can't reach."

Since Banks was a billionaire in his own right it all made sense. "I'm waiting on what it is you want from us."

"My family to be uprooted and placed somewhere beautiful. Where we don't have to worry about money or the struggles of normal people. If you do that, I know of one person who's able to work on aircrafts. He's an Englishman who moved here many years ago. Just like you, his plane had trouble. Except when he landed, he wanted to stay. Walked away from his million-dollar real estate company and everything."

"Sounds like he's doing good. Why would he take the risk?" Banks asked.

Jago smiled. "He does love it here. Learned the language faster than any person not from this country. People were shocked. Some believed he lied and always knew how to speak Spanish."

"You think he'll help us?" Mason responded.

"Yes."

"You don't sound too sure," Banks said.

"It's not that I don't sound sure. It's just that...if he helps us, I have to be willing to give him what he wants."

"And what's that?" Banks responded, leaning closer.

Jago looked out of the window at his beautiful daughter who was tending to the farm. Sweat covered her brow and she was wearing a dress that seemed off occasion for the brutal work. Even under the beat of the sun she was still stunning.

"Wait, this nigga wants your daughter?" Mason questioned.

"Always has. It was the one thing money or learning the language couldn't buy him." He sighed. "Until now."

Banks looked at the beauty. "So, when you go to paradise, she isn't going with you?"

"No. Just me, my sons and my wife."

Banks nodded. "I need to make a call."

"Who are you calling?"

"If I'm going to take up your proposal, I need to make a few moves first. Where is your phone?"

Jago looked at his wife and nodded his head. "Come with me, sir."

While they were gone Mason and Jago spoke about life. He was surprised at how much he liked the man even though he also had ulterior motives.

When Banks returned there was a look of completion on Banks' face that Mason recognized clearly having known the man for most of his life.

He had done something.

He just wished he knew what.

CHAPTER THIRTY-ONE

WALID

"I'm willing to do anything."

Sydney closed the door in the room where Arbella rested. She had been crying nonstop, and all attempts to get the information on where Lance layed his head landed on deaf ears. The Wales' and the Lou's couldn't determine if she was trying to protect her ex, or herself.

Either way, they were growing impatient.

"She's asleep now," Sydney whispered. "I gave her one of my sleeping pills."

Joey placed a hand on her shoulder and said, "Thank you."

"I'm happy to help." He kissed her and she smiled before walking away.

"Them pills getting on my fucking nerves," River said.

"Drop it." Spacey added. "Everybody in this room has been drugged once. You'll be aight."

Walid frowned, having no idea what he was talking about.

Taking a deep breath Joey faced Walid, Spacey, Minnesota, Zercy and River. Shit had definitely gotten kicked up a notch.

Walid said, "Until I find out who this nigga is, she can't know who I am."

"I don't think you should go there." Joey said. "By pretending to be Ace."

"Why not?" Spacey shrugged. "If she's more likely to give us the information if she believes he's Ace, we have to do what we have to do. 'Cuz at this point the fact that she hadn't seen him got me worried. I mean where the fuck is he? Her ex gotta know."

"I agree." Zercy said. "I'm not feeling the whole trick in the bag situation, but we got to use whatever we got at this point. With Banks being on his way the moment he finds out that one of his sons is in danger..."

Everybody shook their heads just considering the possibilities.

"So, what's your plan?" Zercy asked Walid.

He sat down and dragged his hands down his face.

"For two days I hated my brother. And I...I hated him because I let him get in my head and take me from my family."

He was visibly shaken up in a way no one had ever seen. And if it wasn't obvious before, it was obvious now that he loved his girl and son.

"But I left Wales Island with him, and now I gotta make shit right. And the one thing I'm sure about is she is feeling Ace. When I walked into her shop I had intentions of going off. Demanding that she tell me where my brother was. Demanding that she gives me information on her ex. All that went out the window when she looked at me." He looked up at the Wales clan. "She loves my brother. And it may be too early to say, but he chose right."

They sighed.

"She doesn't know anything. So, I have to get her to tell me. And I'm willing to do anything. Even if it means being Ace."

Minnesota and Zercy were sitting on the bed looking at an ambiance video on YouTube. Ironically it showcased a beautiful beach with aqua colored water.

"We must have been tripping." He said listening to the smooth music while viewing the scene.

She laughed. "We actually left a place that looked like that to come back to this. Doesn't make any sense does it?"

"They say you always want what you can't have. It must be true."

Silence filled the room for a second.

Minnesota briefly thought about how badly he fought to get her into his life. Only for them to drift apart now that she had accepted.

"What changed between us?" She asked.

He took a deep breath, and she was relieved. He wasn't much on speaking about his feelings these days. In fact, he appeared nervous whenever the conversation of a relationship reared its head. But with the deep breath she felt at least she was about to get answers.

"I felt like you didn't need me."

She frowned. "I don't understand."

"Before we got on the island, I saw our relationship being different. I saw us spending time together and if we could build a family that would have worked but it wasn't a necessity for me. Because I had you."

She felt as if she were about to cry.

"But the more time we spent there, it...it seemed like you got immersed into your family so much that there wasn't a place for us to have our own."

"That's not true."

"Just listen, baby." He placed a hand over his heart. "I'm talking to you. And I don't know if I'll be able to express myself in this way ever again."

She nodded.

"A nigga got lonely. And when you're lonely you grasp at figures in the past when you can't see a future. And so, I started thinking about being back here and what that would feel like."

She looked down. "As bad as this hurts, I get it."

"With all that said, there's never come a time where I didn't love you. There never came a time where I didn't want to be with you. For all I know I could have willed all of this into my existence."

"What part?"

"Why we're here."

She sighed. "I read in one of the books you used to read that if more than one person has the same desire that gives it power."

He smiled, knowing it to be true.

"You thought being back here would be better." She continued. "Ace thought being back here would be better. Joey clearly longed to be with us. And I'm not entirely sure that Uncle Mason and pops didn't miss it too." She paused. "If you ask me, we all had a part in coming back here."

He nodded. "Now having been here and seeing everything that happened, I realize how great we had it. We didn't have to worry about anything. Since when does having everything become a problem?"

"Maybe we didn't deal with our own shit before we moved." She got up and looked out the window overlooking Joey's garden. "And so, it followed us there."

"What's on your mind, Minnie?"

"For a long time, I resented you."

"Why?"

"I thought it was because of you I couldn't have a child. And it hurt so badly it made me think that perhaps being here would make things easier too." She turned to face him. "You were right when you said the Wales love drama."

"I was just talking." He waved the air.

"But it's true, Zercy." She sat on the bed in front of him. "Maybe we're the kind of family that thrives off of uncertainty. The unknown. And because we chase the unknown so much, we find it in violent ways."

"I'm not going to lie, you're confusing me."

"I do love you. And I do want to be with you. I want the chance to show you what you mean to me. The idea that you had to watch me immerse myself into my family and leave you on that island, breaks my heart. But this is me. This is us. Always living on the edge of danger with the possibility of falling off."

"I get it."

"But can you deal with it?" She placed a hand on the side of his face. "Because I don't think it will ever change for us."

River just entered her apartment when she was shocked to see Tinsley sitting on the sofa. She wasn't surprised that he was inside, but she was surprised that he was there that day.

She tossed her keys on the table by the door and sat next to him. Neither said a word to the other. And yet they were speaking volumes.

"I heard the twins successfully fucked up paradise." Tinsley said.

"Not surprised. They are Wales'." River said. "Them red niggas spoiled as fuck."

"You a ligga too." He joked. "Banks is going to be livid."

"Tell me something I don't know." She looked at him.

"He'll be on his way and when he gets here, I'm sure he will–"

"No, Tinsley, I mean tell me something I really don't know." She glared, on another topic altogether.

Despite the pain of separation, prison appeared to have been good to him. He was still tiny and fit. Without a scar on his face. It wasn't like he should be any different because with the money she and Banks was sending, he should've been king.

"You know, don't you?" He asked. "About Banks?"

"You put on like you didn't have anywhere to go. And now I'm finding out that Banks set you up too. Why would you lie to me?"

"I didn't lie, River."

"But you did though. The apartment. The car. The money. He gave you everything."

He shook his head slowly from left to right. "I'm grateful for Banks. But nothing he could provide me with financially would take the place of being with you. And I know you don't want me but–"

"I'm a lesbian."

"You weren't one when we fucked."

"But I was though. Even everything that happened with us in the hotel room was masculine on my part. You pushing the issue is only going to push me away. Is that what you want?"

He turned his body to see her clearly. "I need to make something clear to you."

"I'm listening."

"I did time for you." Tears rolled down his cheeks. "There were nights where I had to do things to people that I never want to mention again. The only thing that kept me sane was that I knew that when I came back that you would be here waiting. We are together." He squeezed her hands. "Whether you want me or not, that won't change. What will change is how you move about the world. Them bitches that you with are gone."

"Hold up, I-."

"No, you wait a minute! Everything is different now. I'm going to give you some time because with the twins being here, things are about to get dark. So, everybody will need to be on deck. But let's be clear, by time I mean a few days. After that it'll be *time* for you to get with the program. It's you and me and nothing else. Your days of eating pussy are officially over."

With that he stood up and walked out the door.

Walid was standing in Arbella's bedroom doorway. He wanted to see if she was awake when suddenly Joey rushed to the door. Luckily she was still asleep because he yelled, "Walid, you gotta come! Now."

He softly closed the door. "What is you doing? My name is Ace remember?"

"Fuck all that! You have to come now. Things are serious."

Abruptly, Walid was led to the front of Joey's house, on the deck. Spacey, Minnesota, Blakeslee, Zercy and River were already present and watching the horizon.

In the distance were four caravans. They were black and had the letter W inscribed on the back in Heraldry print.

"He's here," Spacey said in a low voice.

Most were too afraid to speak. After all, they were definitely vehicles belonging to their billionaire father. And they were definitely approaching Joey's estate.

When the vehicles parked in front of where they stood, they each waited for Mason and Banks to appear from inside. But what they saw next put them on pause.

First came Riot, followed by Patrick and Bolt.

Having missed them terribly, Blakeslee ran up to them and wrapped her arms around their bodies as they screamed and cheered happily. The others couldn't help but smile and joined in the reunion of joy.

Where were Banks and Mason?

Walid ruffled a few heads, but he waited for who was in the final van before he could breathe easily. Because the first van released his relatives, the second and third released armed men but the fourth van remained closed.

And to be clear, Spacey, Minnesota, Zercy and Joey were waiting too.

Would it reveal Banks and Mason?

Suddenly when the side door opened, Walid felt his legs betray him. Because he was looking into the eyes of his girl and his son.

Overcome with love, he fell to his knees and cried due to the immense sense of relief flooding his heart. Walid wasn't known as an overly emotional cat, so this took everyone by surprise.

With tears running down her face and joy in her heart, Aliyah rushed up to him, and wrapped her arms around him as he bonded with his girl and baby boy.

The family was back together.

But again, where was Banks and Mason?

The family assembled in the living room while Aliyah explained what happened. They were seated on the couch, and she had their undivided attention.

"We had no idea what was happening." She whispered.

She had tried to hand off Baltimore's heavy ass several times, but no one felt like carrying extra weight.

Clearing her throat, and holding him herself she said, "We were in the kitchen preparing for breakfast as usual, when your father's trusted men entered. Said that a plane was waiting for us to bring us here and to leave everything and go immediately. We were worried, but they had the code word your father had given us years ago if anything ever happened."

"Who flew y'all over?" Walid asked.

"The band. Apparently Banks was upset that it was because of them that you all were here." She looked at Walid and back at Joey. "Said that was how they could make things right."

Walid felt guilty but was happy to be reunited with his family.

"So...so where is pops?" Spacey asked.

He asked the best question of the night because everyone for sure wanted to know.

"I don't know. He wasn't with us. It was like he wanted us all to be together. For what, I'm not sure."

They all looked at one another and were more frightened than ever.

In one of Joey's many guestrooms, the baby was asleep as Walid tried to explain to his girl why she couldn't let on that she was his girl. Sitting on the bed, all she heard was her worst fears come to life.

And it caused her great distress.

Whispering he said, "I know this hurts you. But something is wrong with Ace. And she alone holds the information we need."

"But there has to be another way."

"Another way like what?" He whispered. "Because if you know a way I'm all ears."

She looked down and back at him. "I heard the stories. Late at night when Spacey, Minnesota and Mason thought I wasn't listening. It was always over alcohol, but they spoke of tales of violence, death and even torture."

Walid was put off by her callous tone, but he wanted to be sure he understood what she was saying. "Are you suggesting that we do her harm?"

"I'm suggesting that I would have a big problem with her holding or even looking at my man as if he were her own."

He touched her hand. "Nothing will happen other than me convincing her to tell me what she knows.

My father will be here soon. And when he does come, he'll want answers about where Ace is. And right now, none of us have them."

"Do what you have to do." She pulled away. "But if you violate our relationship, I will never speak to you again. And trust me, there are things you don't know about me. One of them is that I can carry a grudge. Do you really wanna see?"

She got up and walked away.

CHAPTER THIRTY-TWO
WALID
"I like it better this way."

It was time to get to work...

Walid sat on the floor in the room Arbella was staying in at Joey's house. Her feet rested next to the pillows by the headboard, while her face lay at the foot of the bed, where she could see Walid whom she still thought was Ace.

Devastation of what happened at her shop, and how it exploded with her inside, was sitting on her like a ton of bricks.

"Someone took my phone," she said.

"No one here took it." He said calmly.

"It doesn't matter, it's password protected, and I don't want to speak to anyone anyway."

"Arbella...finish the story."

She sighed deeply. "When I first got with him I thought he was what I deserved. My father was a known drug dealer who was in and out of prison and my mother was the lady with the burned face. I had some friends but for the most part people avoided me. At least I felt that way inside. But Lance...I thought he was different."

"How did you meet him?" He questioned.

"You don't remember the story of the building? That I told you on the roof of the building that night?"

Walid ran into his first stumbling block.

"With everything going on, please refresh my memory."

"My father was trying one of his many business ventures, in an attempt to make drugs legal. Or wash his money as he says." She paused. "He just came home from prison and saw this apartment building with about ten units inside. He figured with some of the money he saved up he could at least put a down payment on the property and then hustle the rest of the money to make ends meet."

Walid situated himself again on the floor. He was growing impatient, which wasn't his brand. But he wanted to find Ace.

"We went to the building and within a few minutes, Lance came to the property to show us around. From the moment he saw me for some reason he glued himself to me."

"I don't understand."

"My father was the one interested in the property but as we walked around, Lance would show me the different units and speak to me directly as if I had the money."

"So, he been going hard for a minute."

"Hard is an understatement, Ace. At first my father was annoyed by how he was treating him. He figured the prison years that he possessed put some type of smell on his flesh. That would make people not want to be bothered. After a while when it was obvious that it wasn't rejection, but Lance's obsession with me, my father played into it."

"Has your father ever done anything like that before?"

"No. We didn't have much of a relationship back in the day. I would come to see him every now and again, but my loyalty was always with my mother. Until she was burned and put into a coma."

"Why does it sound like you had to choose?"

"Because I thought I did." She sat up yoga style and looked down at him. "When I was about thirteen-years-old my mother and father got into a big argument. To this day she protects me from the truth, and he refuses to talk about it either way."

"Did you ask either of them?"

"I'd beat around the bush. But I'm not the kind of person to pry so I hoped that at some point they would tell me. Needless to say, that never happened."

"Go ahead."

"But I remember more than they think I did."

"About what?"

"What happened to my mother's face." She paused. "One day, my father woke me up in the middle of the night. Carried me in his arms out of my bed and then out the door. I still remember the cold winter air attacking my face and feet, because they weren't protected by my pajamas. Next, he tucked me in his car and blasted the heat so high that the difference in the temperatures shocked my body and scared me. Confused, when he closed the door I watched him rush inside the building again. Suddenly the windows in our apartment glowed."

"Glowed?"

"Fire."

Walid nodded.

"What happened next is why I have been too afraid to ask too many questions. For now, I'll say my mom nearly burned alive. While she was inside screaming, he stood next to the car and looked at the building. Maybe I'm crazy but I could have sworn I saw a smile on his face."

"So, you look like you have your answer."

"About what?"

"What happened to your mother's face."

"The thing is I don't. Without me asking, he told the police that he went into the building to save her. Because he smelled the smoke. He was only able to save me instead. But I replayed that moment back in my mind a million times and I never once smelled smoke before he took me out."

Suddenly she started crying uncontrollably. Her tears were so hard her body convulsed in weird and crazy ways.

"Do you think he was responsible for what happened at your stores?"

She shook her head left to right. "The thing is, I don't know." She cried harder.

Walid told himself that he wouldn't hold her or touch her physically out of respect for Aliyah. But he needed to know what was going on with his brother. And he would do anything to get to the truth.

Even if it meant taking advantage of her vulnerability.

And so, he rose and walked in her direction.

Sitting on the bed, he held her into his arms. Her body melted into him like butter in a hot frying pan. She wanted to feel something outside of the pain she felt in that moment, and he would do just fine.

After all, not only was her shop blown to pieces. But upon looking at the news, she learned her other shops were destroyed too. This was an orchestrated event geared at ruining her life.

Or taking her life.

She couldn't be sure.

In her mind, he was all she had.

Walid got situated on the bed and continued to hold her. She cried into his chest and then looked up at him and kissed his lips. With his back against the headboard, she crawled on top of him and looked him in his eyes.

Removing the gold band that held his curls she said, “I like it better this way.”

He was stiff, and she helped herself by removing her panties and guiding him deep into her body.

Walid could fake if he wanted, but her pussy felt good. Felt right. With his hands on her waist, he pumped in and out of her as the nectar from her pussy fell down the sides of his throbbing dick.

Her head fell backwards and tickled his inner thigh as she eased up and down like a healthy heartbeat. He was delicate, but firm and felt so good she had to look him in the eyes.

“You feel...different.”

He felt himself about to cum upon hearing her words.

“More...passionate.” She paused. “But I like it.” Leaning forward, her mouth covered his until she rested her face in the pit of his neck and moaned softly. The sound vibrated through his body and made exploding into her center easier.

He didn’t stop pumping until he emptied every drop.

With his dick still tucked inside, he said, "I need to know where he lives."

"Who?" She kissed his chest once.

"Lance. And your father." He tucked her hair behind her ear. "Tell me."

"But my father is not involved."

"Arbella, if he torched your mother's building and wanted you with Lance, how can you be sure? I know you don't want to tell me, but I'm involved now. I was in that building too and could've been hurt."

"Ace, I'm scared."

"Do you care about me?"

"Yes," she said with her whole heart, kissing him again. "You know I do."

"And did you see my family on the way inside?"

"Yes, I did." She nodded.

"We are wealthy."

"I understand."

"I don't think you do. My father is one of the biggest billionaires in the world. And he will come soon, asking questions. And if you think your father can be cruel, wait until you meet mine."

She sniffled and looked up at him. "I...I didn't know. That you were wealthy."

"Why?"

"Because of the cheap motel you tried to take me to and–."

Walid laughed. "I had to make sure you were legit. That you didn't know who I was first. And until you give me the information on Lance and your father, I still don't know. You have to choose a side. What will it be? Us or them?"

She thought long and hard and realized if she was going to be safe, and have some semblance of the world she wanted, she needed to be honest.

And so, she rattled off all the details. Lance and her father's. And in the end, he had everything he needed to know.

Slowly he got up and got dressed. Walking to the door he said, "I'm sorry."

Grabbing the covers over her naked body she said, "But...but why?"

He walked out.

Not even two minutes later Joey entered. "Get dressed." He tossed her a new pair of gray sweatpants and a shirt that Blakeslee gave her to wear. They were about the same size.

"What's going on?"

"Get dressed. I won't say it again."

With no care of her naked body, she quickly did as she was told. When she was done, she pulled her knees up to her body and sat against the headboard. "What's happening?"

"The person that just left the room was not Ace."

"I don't understand." She trembled.

"That was Ace's twin brother. Now we're sorry we had to lie to you, but your folks fucked with some really important people. His brother. My brother. Who has been missing for at least two days."

Her eyes widened. "But I didn't know!" She said, shaking her head rapidly from left to right. She thought she was about to pass out at the thought of losing him. "I thought he was avoiding me and–."

"He wasn't."

"I didn't have anything to do with–."

"We believe you. And at the same time that doesn't matter. Things are about to get serious. So, we're going to make you some breakfast. Make sure you're safe. But you can't leave this house. And more importantly you can never tell anybody about what happened between you and Walid tonight."

"Walid?"

"That's Ace's twin's name." He paused. "Am I clear?"

She nodded.

He walked out the door.

CHAPTER THIRTY-THREE
BANKS

"I'd rather do business with Nicolas a million times."

Jago was on his patio with his wife, his daughter, his sons, Mason and Banks drinking punch. From the distance he saw the road come alive with dirt clouds agitated by rolling tires.

Banks and Mason rose slowly.

Jago frowned. "What's happening?" He stood too.

Banks ignored him and within seconds three red pickup trucks pulled in front of the property. Out of the first popped Kordell Fuego. He was from Baltimore but just like so many others, fell in love with Mexico and made his mark.

He was also one of the quietest but powerful drug dealers still operating in the US. Less than five people knew about him.

Banks was one of them.

Mason looked over at Banks. "You said you would never contact him."

Banks remained silent.

"You just sold our souls." Mason continued.

Kordell had been kissed by the sun and so his chocolate skin was so smooth it looked refurbished.

While his dreads hung down his back, the tips were dressed in real gold rings.

Once out of the truck, he bopped up to Banks. "Ah, the Great Mr. Wales," he shook his hand and his skin smelled of fine oil. "I can't believe you called."

The men unloaded from their vehicles and manhandled Jago and his sons to the ground.

"What's going on?" Jago yelled, as his face was smashed into the earth. "We were helping you! Why would you betray us like this?"

"Any man who would sell his daughter for profit, is not a man I trust." Banks said through clenched teeth. "I'd rather do business with Nicolas a million times than to be bothered with a man like you."

"What you don't know is that she loves him! I would have never given the okay otherwise."

Banks and Mason looked at one another. He didn't know, and now it was too late. He judged and was found wanting.

"What now?" Kordell asked Banks.

"Release his sons but keep a hold on them."

Kordell nodded and the men let go, but their guns were still trained on them in case they got frisky.

"I also need you to make sure his sons, wife and daughter are safe." He looked down at Jago. "You can do whatever you want with him. And then get me to the plane."

Kordell said Banks' favorite word. "Done."

As they walked down the road toward one of the trucks Mason looked over at Banks. "I thought you called the kids."

"Nah, they'll see me when they see me."

Mason looked back at Jago who was being led to one truck, while his sons, wife and daughter were being led to another.

All were crying.

"You were wrong for that, Banks."

"Just one man's opinion."

"After all these years, my opinion is the only opinion that counts. And I'm telling you that foul ass move will come back to haunt you."

Banks stopped abruptly. "He still sold his daughter for a way out. And there is nothing more important than my family. Our family. Anybody else can suck my dick."

The moment they pulled up to the airport which held the plane, the mechanics got out and worked diligently on the aircraft. Nicolas' men weren't there after all. Using the resources of the airport, by breaking in, they made immediate strides on repairing the plane.

As they busied themselves, Kordell stood in front of Banks and Mason. And it was evident that Mason couldn't stand the ground he stood on.

"What do you want with my family?" Mason questioned.

"Your family?" Kordell laughed.

"If you think this man is not my family, you are stupider than I thought."

"Still jealous I see."

"What do you want with us?" Mason pressed.

Kordell took a deep breath. "Banks knows." He looked at him and back at Mason. "I'll let him tell you when it's time."

"You don't have a–."

Before they could get their bearings together, they heard the loud broken-down engines of Nicolas' trucks in the distance.

"Get in the aircraft!" Kordell said to them while rushing to alert his men. "We have it from here!"

Without questioning, Banks and Mason rushed inside the plane. When Pilot and Co-Friend were in their positions, the door closed just before one of Nicolas' goons tried to enter.

Gunfire rang from everywhere outside.

But even if a bullet punctured the skin of the airplane, just like commercial aircrafts, it would be no problem to fly. Besides, the airplane was pressurized.

And so, while the war took place on the ground, Banks continued to taxi down the runway as fast as possible to hit the skies.

CHAPTER THIRTY-FOUR

ACE

"There will come a time when you'll regret this shit."

Ace was in the worst pain of his life in the empty warehouse basement in Baltimore.

In fact, prior to traveling to and arriving in the states, he was shielded so much that he had never been in any pain ever. But it was obvious that for reasons Ace didn't know, that Lance wanted to see him tortured.

And at this point it hurt so badly, Ace wondered if death wouldn't be better.

He had already jabbed him in the gut with the tip of a hot steel rod. And now he was cutting up his perfect face with small but deliberate scars.

Having sat in his own urine, he asked for the hundredth time, "What do you want with me?"

"Believe it or not, I'm not going to kill you." Lance laughed.

This was news.

"Why not?"

"Because I want her to see what I've done to you. She may think she doesn't have a vain bone in her body, but she does, and will never be able to accept you like this."

"So, you're going to disfigure me?" Ace yelled. With his good looks gone, he didn't see any way possible that he could be happy. "Just kill me if that's what you're going to do."

"The fact that you don't want to live, makes what I'm about to do even better."

Ace was enraged. "Leaving me alive may be the stupidest shit you've ever done in your life."

"Says the nobody."

"If only you knew who I was."

"Now this is getting interesting." Lance continued as he placed another tiny scar on his face, just to see the blood trickle from his flesh. He had done it so much that it was as if Ace's skin was immune to the pain. It hurt so badly that he went numb a long time ago.

"There will come a time when you'll regret this shit."

"You're very arrogant. If you knew how much money me and my family have you wouldn't be."

Ace laughed.

"Fuck is so funny?" Lance questioned.

"Your money."

"Broke niggas would think it's hilarious. But trust me, without capital and your looks she will have nothing to do with you. I even blew up her shops. She will come running back to me. But this time, the price will be heavy."

"No matter what you do to me, it's a fact that she will still be on my dick."

"That's a bet I'm willing to wager."

When Lance's phone rang he grew worried when he saw his father, Satchel's, name on the screen. His father didn't call him much, so it wasn't a call he could ignore.

In his father's opinion he gave him enough money to be able to care for himself and so his work was done. They did not have the regular familial bond.

Stepping away from Ace he looked at his men, "Keep him quiet."

They stood on the left and right of him and one pressed his hand so close to Ace's mouth, his teeth hurt.

When he thought it was safe he said, "Father."

"Are you stupid?"

He frowned. "What do you mean?"

"Do you have Ace Wales in your possession?"

There was no way on earth he was going to tell him the truth. After all, he didn't understand how he knew in the first place.

"I don't know what you're talking about, father."

"I don't know where you are or what you're doing but the world is crashing down around us right now, Lance! Valentine has gone into hiding. No one knows where Arbella is and several of my businesses have been met with people in business suits asking questions. Took me some time but after a while I found out what it was all about. You are causing trouble for me once again."

"Father, I–."

"So, I'm going to ask you once more, do you have the Billionaire's son Ace Wales in your possession?"

A billionaire?

Lance looked at Ace and his knees buckled. Earlier, he ordered Arbella's father to find more information about him, and he came up short. So he figured he was a nobody.

He was wrong.

He had never seen a billionaire's son in his life. And he definitely didn't think that Ace was of that breed.

Suddenly it made sense why he was so cocky. But what shocked him, was that he never once told him who he was. Instead, he took to letting himself be destroyed.

Lance looked at Ace's bloodied face punctured with small wounds. He looked at his gut which was bleeding. He reasoned that if it were true, that he grabbed the son of a man whose riches exceeded his, that life as he knew it would be over.

His father may even strip him of his wealth.

And so, he decided to lie. "No, I don't father."

"Come to me in fifteen minutes." Suddenly he heard the timer in the background that his father always set when he was serious about punctuality. "We have a lot to discuss about you, my money and that girl Arbella."

Ace looked at him and smiled. He wasn't sure what was said on the call, but he was certain by the horror on his face that he now knew he was the subject.

When he dropped the phone in his pocket he nodded for them to release his mouth.

"What were you saying about money again?" Ace asked.

There was nothing left to do. Lance would have to kill Ace to keep his secret. And he would deal with whatever came later.

Looking at his man behind Ace he said, "Do what you got to do. And then dump the body."

Ace took a deep breath.

This wasn't how he saw things ending but so be it. His only hope was that at some point his father and family would avenge his death.

He had officially gotten too close to the sun and was drowning.

Suddenly the windows came crashing in with fire laced rocks. Next there were the sounds of fractured wooden doors all around.

Somebody else was there!

"Fuck him! Protect me!" Lance told his goons.

As armed men came rushing down the stairs, Lance's men fired in all directions. Most of them were covered in black but there were several who weren't. One of them was Zercy.

"Over here!" Ace called across the way upon spotting him. "Hurry!"

Zercy ran toward him, but for his efforts received a bullet to the middle of the forehead.

He died instantly as blood poured from his skull.

Ace's jaw dropped, as he fought with what was happening. Did he see a man whose face he saw almost every day, lying lifeless on the floor?

Before he could process what was occurring, his brother Spacey came into view next.

As bullets continued to fly around and the walls burned, Spacey didn't see Ace across the large room. But he did see Zercy's body on the floor.

"Fuck!" Spacey quickly went to help but was struck with a bullet to the chest.

Now Ace felt dizzy.

The Wales family members were being annihilated right before his eyes. In an attempt to save his life.

Realizing that two Wales men were hit, two of the armed men in the Wales' camp dragged Zercy and Spacey out of the building.

Ace felt nauseous.

Prior to that moment he only wanted to play gangsta. And now, just like Lance, the two little rich boys realized what being gangsta really meant.

Bullet after bullet rang out.

And Lance, fearing for his life, managed to escape from a destroyed window above.

If Ace survived he would find him, no matter where he hid. That he promised. And then suddenly he saw Walid.

"Brother! Are you here?!" Walid asked through the smoke.

When Ace saw his twin across the way his heart rocked. If something happened to him, like it happened to Spacey he would rather die.

"Get out!" Ace coughed. "Leave! Now! Please!"

From across the way Walid finally saw him. Unfortunately for him, he didn't see the man behind him. And so, Walid was struck over the back of his head with a bat.

Once and then twice.

Blood spurted everywhere, and Ace felt faint.

Seeing his brother go out forced him to reconcile with the guilt in a way he never knew existed. This was all his doing.

After bashing his brother, the stranger moved toward Ace, and after witnessing what happened to Walid, he was happy he was next. In his opinion he didn't deserve to live after his twin went down. They may have argued but doing life without him was not possible.

In a quest to have an adventure, blood poured from his brothers and Zercy.

The man was almost upon Ace until suddenly he was shot from behind. There was so much smoke that Ace couldn't see who was involved.

Suddenly two men in all black approached Ace.

Were they Lance's men or his? He got his answer when he was untied and lifted off the chair.

Once outside he saw his father.

He saw Banks Wales.

And he passed out.

CHAPTER THIRTY-FIVE
ACE
"You can't isolate what's a part of you."

Ace looked down at his feet nestled in the golden sand. He smiled as the warm aqua green water lapped at his toes. Raising his arms out to his sides, he exhaled and breathed in the healing air surrounding his body.

It was all a dream.

He had never left Wales Island.

And his brothers, Walid, Spacey and Zercy were all safe.

As he basked in the glory, suddenly the sun was covered with what looked like a black sheet. It was so dark; he couldn't see his hands before his face. Instantly, the air grew suffocating, and it was as if he were in a funhouse with air inflated walls that pressed against him.

He couldn't breathe.

Dripping with sweat, when he popped up, he was in bed with all types of hospital equipment connected to his body. And when he touched his face he could see it was covered with bandages, mummy style.

Looking down at his stomach, that wound that was inflicted due to the iron prod was patched up too.

Laying back down, rage consumed him.

He was angry he survived, and his brothers didn't. Angry that he would have to live with knowing their deaths was all his fault. And there was nothing he could do about it.

Zercy once said that guilt was more poisonous to man than any drug, alcohol or toxin could ever be.

He reasoned, the way he felt, he was right.

Opening his eyes wider, when he looked to his right he saw Walid staring at him from bed. The top of his head was bandaged, and he had a saline bag connected to his arm. But for the most part he was fine.

Just that quickly a huge weight lifted off Ace's heart and he wept. The bandages caught every drop. Every tear. It was a hard cry. The type that you only received after thinking the worst while receiving the best.

His brother, his closest friend, was alive.

When he was done, Walid asked, "Was it worth it?"

"I'm so sorry, man I didn't know all of this would happen."

"Our brother-in-law is dead. Men won't return to their families. And all of this happened because you wanted what you wanted. But then again that's always the case, isn't it?"

"It's not that I didn't want what we had, I just wanted something different. Had I known you would have been hurt then I would have chosen otherwise."

"Would you have really? Do you know that had it not been for father coming when he did, that I wouldn't be here either? What would that have done to Baltimore? To be raised without his father."

The guilt was too great and so he got mad. "But now you don't have to worry about that."

"I'm a father. I'll always have to worry about that."

"Do you think I wanted this to happen? Do you think I wanted you to be hurt? I never asked you to come."

Was Walid hearing things? "Excuse me?"

"I never asked you to come. You're your own man."

"Not only did you ask me to come but you begged me to. And I abandoned my girl and my son to be at your side. But I promise you something, and I want you to hear me clearly. I will never ever choose you again."

"The way you coming at me it's like you want to be enemies."

"If that will keep you the fuck away from me then so be it."

"You can't isolate what's a part of you."

"Watch me."

"This is the wrong thing we should be doing right now." Spacey said from across the room.

Upon seeing his face, once again Ace felt relief. "I'm sorry. I didn't–"

"That's the thing about regrets. They're always done after the damage. At the same time, I was reckless before too. He moaned, touching his chest which was bandaged up. "And I forgive you." He paused. "The best part is now I can tell you both apart."

It wasn't until that moment that Ace realized that they were in a large hospital room. It looked like it was built for six people but at the moment it was only for the Wales boys.

"Anyway, if I were you I would concern myself more with pops." Spacey warned.

His heart rocked. "Where is he?"

"On his way up now," Mason said from the seated position on the left.

The place was so large, and the bandages so thick, that Ace couldn't take the whole room in at once, and so he didn't see him either.

Suddenly the door opened, and Banks entered, flanked by four men. He always had security, but it was extra beefed-up now. After all, he was in America. In fact, in the hallway they lined the walls as if they were guarding the president himself.

Walking up to Ace's bedside he looked down at him. The expression on his face was so evil it made Ace's heart skip a beat.

"What the fuck is wrong with you, boy?"

"Father, I didn't–"

"Because of you, Minnesota doesn't have a husband. Because of you all of us are here instead of on our Island. What was so wrong with being in peace?"

Suddenly the cockiness Ace once possessed was tapped on. If everybody was going to hate him, it was easier being the bad guy than it was being sorry. And so, he looked at each one of them and said, "I'm sick of apologizing. This my life and my world and I can do whatever I want to do."

Banks laughed hard.

"Your world?" He moved so close to the bed it rocked. "The blood in your veins is mine. The texture of your hair is mine. The smoothness of your skin is mine. The very air you breathe in this room belongs to me and was only possible by my grace. I am the god that has allowed you to live. To thrive. To eat and to sleep. I control every dollar that has ever come to you. All that's left is worthless. So, you two niggas," he looked at Walid, "are the gods of everything else." He focused back on Ace.

Mason lowered his head, having seen this type of mood from Banks before.

Shit had gotten serious.

Walid felt bad because he knew why his father was upset with him. He should have never allowed Ace's desire to play in the darkness, to take him away from the light.

"It appears you've gotten your wish, Ace." Banks said sarcastically. "To get here I had to do favors for people I don't respect. But if it means saving everyone else I'm willing to do that. We're staying here a bit longer."

Mason looked down.

Spacey shook his head.

"But let me be clear, you will not get another dime from me. You will get no help from me. If you're hungry I won't do as much as give you a biscuit. There is nothing you could say or do that will make me change my mind until I'm sure that this selfishness that is so strong within you is gone."

He stripped the *I Am God* chain off his neck.

Ready to wage war, Ace popped up straight, but Banks took the palm of his hand, covered his face and slammed him back to the bed.

He was about to take the bracelet too when Walid said, "Please, father, don't!"

Ace's fist was clutched, and all present wondered what he would do next.

"Blakeslee gave it to him." Walid continued. "Let him have it."

Banks dropped the half a million-dollar diamond chain in his pocket and let him keep the bracelet.

Mason decided to speak his position later.

Banks turned to face the room. "Anybody that goes against me is cut off. Indefinitely."

He waited for opposition and when none came, he walked out.

Now it was Mason's turn.

First he walked over to Walid and touched his head softly. Then he walked over to Ace whose breath was rapid due to being angry.

"You're going to let him do that to me?" Ace said, eyes red with fury.

"Before we left the island, to come here, Banks had five hundred thousand dollars in Belize currency delivered to the farmer and the daughter you took in the towel shack."

Ace swallowed the lump in his throat.

"Do you know what happened?"

Ace shook his head no.

"It was returned. By the same men. Every cent."

Silence.

"If it is true, that the girl wanted to make a come up off of you, by faking rape, why didn't she or her father, accept the money?"

"I...I'm–."

"You wanted to know how it feels to leave paradise. To not be bothered with family." Mason glared. "Now you'll see."

He walked out too.

EPILOGUE
TWO MONTHS LATER

The sun was high as Arbella sat in her car, on the side of the road next to a park. Her cell phone was in her lap, and she had been waiting on a call for two hours. The person was late, and she feared that she had been given the runaround once again.

Realizing the call would never come, she placed her car in drive, in preparation to pull off after a mother strolled her baby out of her path.

RING.

Throwing the car in park, she fumbled with the phone which fell on the floor under the steering wheel. After what seemed like forever, finally she was in control of the phone again.

And then...*RING. RING.*

"Hello...hello."

Silence.

"Hello!" She said anxiously.

"I was about to hang up."

She breathed deeply. "Thank you for not doing that." She paused. "But what took you so long?"

"Father doesn't want me to have a cell phone," Blakeslee said. "I told you. So, I have to sneak. Luckily for you it's something I'm good at."

She nodded. "I still don't know how you managed to put the cell phone number in the gray sweats Joey gave me to wear."

"Push gave me the phones I asked for. He thinks I'm going to do things to him. I kept one phone myself and gave the other to Ace when I saw him at the hospital. But I gave you my number before everything went down, in case you saw Ace before I did."

"Are you?"

"What?"

"Going to do things to him for the phones?"

Silence.

Arbella sighed, "Please tell me you have what I asked for."

"I do." She paused. "But I asked if he wanted to see anybody, and he said no."

"Did you tell him it was me?"

"No."

Arbella looked down and ahead. "So, why are you doing this if he doesn't want to be bothered?"

"Because he's alone. I'm not there. And I don't want him to be alone. I hear it in his voice. Go see my brother. Give him a hug for me. Please."

Less than ten minutes later, Arbella was in a small town in Baltimore county. When she happened upon a five-floor apartment building, in a run-down area, she wondered if the information was correct.

After parking her car, she walked toward the building and pulled the door open. Slowly she moved to number 3B on the third floor. The space was cramped. Surprisingly enough, the hallway smelled of pine sol and disinfectant.

Someone cared for the building for sure.

Taking a deep breath, she knocked three times on the door. When no one answered, she knocked again.

"Who is it?"

Hearing his voice made her heart rock. "It's me, Ace. Open the door."

"Go away."

"I will come to this building every day for the rest of my life until you let me in." She hung her purse from the crease of her arm and placed two palms on the door. "Please, Ace. Let me inside."

Silence.

Ready to cause a problem for his neighbors she yelled, "Ace, open the–."

CLICK. CLACK.

She knew the door was open because she heard it unlock, but it was she who would have to enter.

When the door was ajar, she was shocked by how dark it was inside. Through one partially open window in the far corner, she saw a recliner and a silhouette of a man sitting on the chair in front of the window.

She knew it was him.

Closing the door behind herself, she locked it and stood in the middle of the floor. "Why did you do that to me? You said you would never leave me, and you did just that."

Silence.

"Ace."

He sighed, and she wished she could see his face. "I look different, and I have nothing to offer you anymore."

Slowly she moved toward him. "I don't care what you—."

"Stay there, Arbella!" He said angrily. "I'm serious."

She didn't listen.

Instead, she continued to walk toward him, until she was standing directly in front of him. Now, with the little light that came through from the window, she could see his face. It was cut up in so many places, it put her on pause.

And still, she didn't care.

"Satisfied?" He asked, hair just as wild as ever.

She moved closer, eased between his legs and got on her knees. Touching his face she said, "I don't care what you look like, Ace. You're still the finest man I've ever known."

He grabbed her wrist and squeezed before throwing her hand away. "Don't play games with me."

"Nigga, do you know what I had to endure to get your address? I had to listen to your little sister tell me boring ass stories for hours! It was horrible! You think I'm gonna let some scars keep me from the only man...the only man..." She looked down.

"The only man what?"

"That I ever wanted." She stared up at him with tears in her eyes. "I love you. And I know it's been a short time, but I don't care what you look like, Ace. I just wanna...I just wanna be with you."

He looked away and then looked back at her. "How do I know you're being honest?"

She dug in her purse and pulled out a cashier's check. "This is the money from the insurance policy from my stores blowing up. Blakeslee told me your father cut you off. And I want you to have it." She handed it to him. "All of it. Every dime."

He threw his head back in the high back recliner, looked up at the ceiling and placed a hand in his face, before squeezing his eyes. It was evident that he was overcome with emotion and didn't want her to see.

She was wise to leave him alone.

Finally looking down at her he said, "I was right about you."

"I don't understand."

"I knew you were the one for me and I was right."

She smiled.

"But I'm not broke." He folded her check and handed it back. "Put this in your purse."

She frowned and did as she was told. "I don't understand."

Suddenly someone walked from the back of the apartment and said, "Ace, my father and I are leaving. Our ride is–."

Arbella, with a puzzled gaze, rose when she saw the beautiful woman. She was from Belize, and she had a heart tattoo on her wrist.

"I'm sorry," the woman said. "I didn't know you had company."

Arbella glared. "Who are you?"

Suddenly an older gentleman exited the room too. "Let's go, honey," he said to the woman as he nodded at Ace, smiled at Arbella and walked out the door.

"Ace, what's going on?"

He pulled her hand softly and she sat on his lap.

"I have been trying to get back here all my life. I may have been young, but I knew that staying on an island was not for me. So, before my eighteenth birthday I made sure to convince my fathers to allow a band I really didn't like, from America, to perform for our party. I always knew they would be my ticket off of Wales Island. And I was right.

"But my plan started way earlier than that. First with learning my father's business. He unknowingly showed me many of his overseas accounts. I learned more about banking and cryptocurrency than he even knew. With a few clicks, I made sure to transfer a few thousand from all of his accounts to another account that I created. That account is now worth ten million dollars."

Her eyes widened.

"After making sure the funds were set up, I knew I needed a way for my father to disown me. I figured rape would be a good way. And so, me, the girl you just saw, her father and an official on the island, faked the crime. Fake blood. Scratches and everything. I knew my pops was a victim of sexual abuse before as a kid, and I figured this would for sure make them kick me off the island. And then I would be free."

"So, them people who left helped?"

He nodded yes. "And for their assistance, I paid them handsomely from the account, and arranged for the band to bring them here too."

She was stunned.

"But the rape still didn't work. Father just punished me and confined me to my room. So, I convinced Walid to come. Knowing that eventually the entire family would be in a place where my father never wanted to return. Then he would hate me. Then he would let me go."

"And it worked," She said softly. "Magnificent lies just to be free."

He grinned.

"So, he finally wrote you off."

"Not really." He tapped her leg once and she rose. Walking over to the window, he pushed a curtain to the side. "Come."

She did.

"See that red car right there?"

She saw a vehicle tucked behind some trees.

"I think they are my father's men." He sat back down, and she sat on his lap. "So, still I'm not free. But soon, everything I dreamed of will come to me. Starting with you."

She didn't know whether to be scared or turned on. "Do you like her? The girl with the heart tattoo on her wrist?"

"No. She's the kind of woman you put in your bed, not on your arm. But you are."

They kissed and she hugged him tightly.

"Oh, I almost forgot something." She reached in her purse and pulled out the *I AM GOD* chain.

"Where did you get this?" He asked, with widened eyes.

"Blakeslee. Before they let me leave, while you were in the hospital still, Banks came to Joey's house. She saw him with the chain, took it and gave it to me. Said it belonged to you and said she wanted me to give it to you."

Ace loved his little sister even more behind that shit.

She was a rider.

"Can I put it on? Where it belongs."

He nodded and she rose, before putting it on his chest.

Straddling him she placed cool hands on the side of his face. "Now what do you want to do?"

"Outside of fucking you, it's time to take over the world."

Are you looking to build your Book Empire?

Do you have trouble marketing your book?

Are you having trouble with your story ideas?

Visit:
www.theelitewritersacademy.com

For Planners, Courses and Templates